A MUZ

"I didn't call you a dog," Clint told him. "I said you had a dog's name."

"You got a smart mouth, mister. Who are you, another sodbuster? I'm gonna give you some of what your friend had last time."

Dicky Parker went for his gun, but as he started to take it out of its holster Clint put his hand over it. At the same time he drew his own gun and jammed the barrel beneath the other man's chin.

"If I pull the trigger," Clint said, "the top of your head is going to heaven, while the rest of you goes to hell."

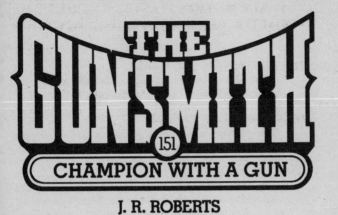

THE GUNSMITH

151

CHAMPION WITH A GUN

J. R. ROBERTS

JOVE BOOKS, NEW YORK

CHAMPION WITH A GUN

A Jove Book / published by arrangement with the author

PRINTING HISTORY
Jove edition / July 1994

ISBN: 0-515-11409-X

A JOVE BOOK®
Jove Books are published by The Berkley Publishing Group,
200 Madison Avenue, New York, New York 10016.
JOVE and the "J" design are trademarks belonging to Jove Publications, Inc.

PRINTED IN THE UNITED STATES OF AMERICA

10 9 8 7 6 5 4 3 2 1

THE GUNSMITH

151

CHAMPION WITH A GUN

ONE

It was a stupid thing to do.

As soon as Clint Adams stepped down from his horse, the heel of his boot snapped. He felt his ankle twist and knew he was hurt.

It was stupid because Clint was usually a man who took great care. He couldn't remember the last time he had a boot heel simply snap.

He staggered from the pain and nearly fell. The only thing that kept him on his feet was hanging onto the massive neck of his big, black gelding, Duke. The big horse, sensing Clint's dilemma, remained still.

"Shit," Clint said, reaching down to rub his ankle through his boot. When that did no good, he gingerly lowered himself to the ground and sat on his butt.

The ankle was throbbing, so he was sure he

had sprained it. He knew that if he took off his boot now he'd never be able to get it back on. On the other hand, if he left it on, it would have to be cut off if the ankle swelled.

He sat there for a few moments until the pain subsided. When he stood up, he thought that perhaps he had been mistaken. The ankle was not sprained, only twisted. He dispelled that myth rather quickly, however, when he put his weight on that foot. The pain was so intense he cried out, reached for Duke's neck, and held on. The ankle began to throb again, and sweat broke out on his brow. He decided that the only thing to do was mount up and find help—hopefully in the person of a doctor.

Mounting up would not be as easy as it sounded. Since his left foot was the one that was hurt, he couldn't put it in the stirrup. It wouldn't hold his weight. On the other hand, if he put his right foot into the stirrup, with his left foot on the ground, the left leg would not hold his weight.

He hobbled around to the other side of Duke and mounted from the wrong side. Using his arms he hauled himself far enough off the ground to get his right foot into the stirrup, and then mounted up properly.

"Okay, Big Boy," he said, taking up Duke's reins, "I was dumb enough to hurt myself, now let's go and find someone who can help."

He was riding for about an hour, his foot throbbing painfully, when he saw the smoke from a fire. Actually, it was smoke from several fires. He decided to head in that direction. Even if it wasn't a town, it might be a settlement or a camp, and if it was large enough to need more than one fire, it might be large enough to have a doctor.

He went that way and soon found himself following the flow of a stream. It eventually led him to a large area that looked to be a cross between a campsite and a settlement. There were a few tents and some ramshackle huts among them. The smoke was coming from three fires and the chimney of the largest wooden structure, which could almost be called a house.

As he approached, several men looked up and saw him, and rushed toward him. He thought they were coming to question him, or help him, until he saw the guns.

"Hey, wait—" he called.

"Just stand easy, mister," one of the men said. All three men were pointing guns at him by now.

Behind them a commotion had started in camp, probably because of him. Some women and children appeared, and from the house two women came into view. Some more men started to come toward them, but they were not carrying weapons.

"What's going on?" he asked.

"Just turn your horse around, mister, and ride on out." The spokesman was holding a rifle, while the other two men were holding worn pistols. Clint didn't think he had to worry about the men with the pistols. The guns looked as though they'd blow up in their hands before they fired properly.

The rifle, though, looked to be in proper working order.

The spokesman was staring at him hard, but did not appear to be a hard man. His features were mild, though lined from years in the sun. He was tall, but slight, almost sickly, with wispy brown hair that moved a bit in the soft breeze.

"I need help."

"Go and get help from your own kind," the man said, jerking the barrel of the rifle.

"And who might that be?"

"As if you don't know."

"No, I don't know. Why don't you tell me?"

Beyond the men, the women and children were coming closer, no longer able to hold back their curiosity. He saw that the two women from the house were actually a woman and a girl—probably mother and daughter, given the resemblance.

"You tryin' to tell us you ain't one of Peck's men?" the spokesman asked.

"Who's Peck?"

One of the other men said, "Dave Peck is the biggest lumberman in the county, that's all."

"And you work for him," a third man said.

"Well, I'm sorry to disappoint all of you nice folks, but I don't work for Dave Peck. In fact, I don't even know Dave Peck."

"Then what are you doing here?" the first man asked.

"I told you, I'm in need of a little help."

Before any of the men could speak, the woman from the house did.

"What kind of help?"

Clint looked past the three armed men toward the woman. She was a handsome woman in her late thirties, her face also lined from constant exposure to the elements. The lines, however, could not detract from the fact that she was still attractive. Not a beauty, but certainly attractive enough.

"Ma'am, it seems I went and did a dumb thing."

"And what was that?"

"I twisted my ankle."

"How bad?"

"Bad enough that I can't walk on it. I think the darned thing has swelled up in my boot."

"Must be sprained then," the woman said. "Andrew, let the man through."

"Iris, we don't know who he is—" the first man protested.

"Did anybody bother to ask before you pointed guns at him?"

"Well . . . no . . ."

"What's your name mister?" she asked.

"Clint Adams."

"Why are you here?"

"I was just riding past when I dismounted to check my horse's hoof. Seems his foot was fine, but my boot heel snapped and I twisted my ankle."

"And you don't work for Peck?"

"Never heard of him."

"My name is Iris McCain. That fool pointing the rifle at you is Andrew Ludlum. Andrew, let the man pass so I can look at his ankle."

"Iris—"

"And put the silly gun away." She looked at Clint and said, "Ride up to my house, mister, and I'll have a look."

"Thank you, ma'am. That's very kind of you."

Clint rode forward, and the three men got out of his way. As he passed, he heard someone speak.

"That woman sure has you henpecked, Lud."

"Shut up, Lem."

"When you gonna marry her?"

"I said . . ."

Clint rode out of earshot and followed the woman up to the house.

TWO

Clint needed some help once he dismounted. Two men supported him and carried him toward the house, while a third man took charge of Duke and said he'd see that the horse got fed.

"Appreciate it," Clint said.

"That's a good-looking animal, mister."

The speaker was the young girl, who looked to be about fifteen.

"Thank you."

The men carried him into the house, followed by the girl.

"Sit him down over here by the table," Iris instructed the men.

They took him to a chair and settled him into it.

"Thank you, boys."

One of the men looked at her and said, "Sure

you don't want us to stay, Iris?"

"I'll be fine, George. Just go on outside and back to your work."

George exchanged a worried glance with the other man, then shrugged and jerked his head. They both left the house, leaving Clint there with Iris and the young girl.

"Is this your daughter?" Clint asked.

"I'm sorry, I'm being rude," Iris said. "Yes, this is my daughter Olivia."

"Livvy," the girl said.

"Hello, Livvy. My name's Clint."

"I'm afraid I have to insist that she call you Mr. Adams," Iris said sternly. "It's respectful."

"I see. Well, all right. I'm all for respect . . . Mrs. McCain."

"Would you like some coffee?"

"Please."

"Olivia, get Mr. Adams a cup while I tend to his ankle."

"Yes'm."

Iris McCain came over to the table and squatted down in front of him.

"Which ankle?"

"The left."

She reached down and touched his left boot gingerly, but confidently.

"Whatever ailments come up around here I usually take care of," Iris told him.

She pressed on his ankle and he flinched.

"You were right on both counts," she said.

"Excuse me?"

"It's sprained, and it's swollen."

"I said it was twisted, you said it was sprained."

She looked up at him and said, "It doesn't matter who said it was sprained, it is."

He smiled and said, "You're right, it doesn't matter. How do we get that boot off?"

"We're going to have to cut it."

He closed his eyes and said, "There goes a perfectly good boot."

"It doesn't have a heel."

"That could have been fixed. Once you cut it, I'll need a new pair."

"We're not so far from Lordsburgh. You'll be able to go there and buy a pair."

"All right, then, cut it off."

Iris looked up at him and said, "Don't be such a baby about it."

She went and got a large kitchen knife and came back. Livvy put a cup of coffee at Clint's elbow.

"Thanks, Livvy."

Iris made a face. Her daughter's name was Olivia. That was what she called her, and that was what she wished everyone would call her.

"Cream?" Livvy asked.

"No, thank you."

Iris got down on her knees and placed the blade of the knife underneath Clint's boot. She had to push his pants leg up to mid-calf to do it.

She looked up at him and asked, "You want a bullet to bite on?"

"Very funny. Go ahead and cut."

She applied pressure, and the sharp knife split the boot cleanly. She cut it all the way down to the ankle, being careful not to jab him with the tip. When that was done she put the knife down, lifted his foot, and gingerly slid the boot off. Using the knife again, she cut the sock off instead of rolling it off.

"Why'd you do that?" he asked.

"Ruined a pair of boots," she said, "what's a sock or two?"

Clint looked at Olivia and asked, "Is your mother always this way?"

"Sometimes she's worse," Livvy said with a broad smile. "She gives Andrew fits."

"Olivia!"

Livvy blushed and looked away.

"Is Andrew your husband, ma'am?"

"No, he's not."

"Oh . . . ow!"

She was probing his ankle with her right hand, while holding his foot in the palm of her left.

He assumed that meant, "Mind your own business."

THREE

"You should have soaked this as soon as it happened," Iris McCain said.

Clint was sitting with his foot in a tub of cold water. His leg was cold up to his knee, and it felt as if it were still creeping up his leg.

"This is not going to do very much good now," she told him.

"Then why do it?"

She stared at him and said, "Because it can't do any harm either."

Clint looked at Olivia and said, "Could you get me another cup of coffee, please?"

"Sure."

She hurried to the stove and then back with it, putting it right at his elbow.

"Thank you, sweetheart."

Olivia smiled, but it was cut short by her mother's words.

"I'd rather you didn't call her that."

Clint looked at Olivia.

"Her name is Olivia, or Livvy, if you must. Please call her by her name."

"I'm sorry, Mrs. McCain," Clint said. "I meant no disrespect."

"Olivia," Iris said, "get me a cup of coffee, please . . . and then go and do your chores."

"Aw, Momma—"

"Do as I say."

Olivia got her mother a cup of coffee, but not with quite the same speed she'd gotten Clint his.

"Chores," Iris reminded her.

"I'll see you later, Mr. Adams."

"All right, Livvy. Thanks."

She waved and went out the door.

"Why was I greeted by men with guns, Mrs. McCain?" Clint asked when the girl was gone.

"Because that's the way men think they have to solve every problem," Iris said. "With guns."

"All men?"

"Yes, Mr. Adams, all men."

"Not me."

"All the men I've met, then."

"You've met me."

She stared at him for a moment, then said, "I notice you wear a gun."

"That's right."

"Why?"

"For protection."

"Against what?"

"Against whatever," Clint said, "and whoever."

"Other men, right?"

"Sometimes."

"When?"

"When need be."

"And when is that?"

"Mrs. McCain," Clint said, "why do I get the feeling you don't like guns?"

"I do not."

"Do you understand their necessity?"

She hesitated, then said, "I do not understand the necessity for men to use them against each other."

"What about hunting?"

"That can be accomplished with a rifle."

"Do you see a difference between pistols and rifles?" he asked.

"When men strap pistols to their hips, they're like little boys. They feel the need to prove themselves."

"You seem to have all men figured out, Mrs. McCain."

Grudgingly, she said, "Not all. . . ."

"What about Andrew—what's his last name a-gain?"

"Ludlum."

"What about him? Do you have him figured out?"

She seemed about to answer, then thought better of it. Instead she said, "You asked why they met you with guns. I'm afraid I didn't give you the answer you were looking for."

"What answer would that be, Mrs. McCain?"

"We've been having trouble with Dave Peck and his men," she said.

"What sort of trouble?"

"Mr. Peck wants us to move."

"To where?"

"He doesn't care where to," she said, "only that we move away from here."

"Why? Is this his land?"

"No . . . not legally."

"What's that mean?"

"He says it's his, but he doesn't legally own it."

"I see . . . I think. Why don't you all just move someplace else?"

She looked at him as if he'd just suggested she might sprout wings and fly off.

"Because this is where we've decided to make our homes."

"You couldn't decide to make them somewhere else, on some other land?"

"We've moved around entirely too much as it is, Mr. Adams. It's time we stopped."

"And this is the place to stop?"

"Yes."

"Have you all decided this?"

"Yes."

"Or have you decided for everyone?"

She glared at him.

"What makes you think I can decide anything for the others?"

"You strike me as a strong-willed woman, Mrs. McCain," Clint said.

"What would you know of my will? You don't even know me."

"I'm just going by what I've seen so far."

"You are quick to judge, Mr. Adams."

"I am not judging, Mrs. McCain."

"Then what would you call it?"

"Observing," he said. "I'm just observing."

"And what do you observe?"

He studied her for a moment.

"You'll get insulted."

She hesitated, then said, "I won't."

"You won't kick me out with a wet, bare foot?"

She stifled a smile and said, "No, I will not."

"Then I can speak freely?"

"Yes," she said, and then added, "but only to observe, not to judge."

"Very well, then."

FOUR

"You're hard on your daughter."

"I don't think—"

"Remember," Clint said, cutting her off, "you said I could observe."

Iris sat back and compressed her lips tightly.

"She's what—fifteen?"

"Yes."

"Almost a woman, I'd say."

"I would not."

"Then let's talk about you."

"What about me?"

"And Andrew."

She remained silent. Clint wondered how he had gotten himself into this. At least the water wasn't as cold. When he'd first put his foot in the water, it had been so swollen he'd been unable to move his toes. He sensed some movement now, though.

"I believe Andrew loves you. Is that true?"

"I don't know."

"Come on, Iris—can I call you Iris?"

"Why not?"

"Surely you know when a man's in love with you."

She hesitated, then said, "I suppose he is."

"In fact, he's asked you to marry him, hasn't he? On several occasions."

Her eyes widened.

"How did you know—did someone tell you that?"

"No, I'm just observing, remember?"

"I don't think I like your observations."

"Because they're accurate?"

"Because they're impertinent."

He smiled.

"Which means they're accurate."

She remained silent.

"Why won't you marry him?"

"That is none of your affair."

"Is he not good enough for you?"

"Andrew is a wonderful man," she said defensively. "He's kind and gentle; he's the least violent man I've ever known."

"Which explains why he was pointing a gun at me, I suppose?"

"He's just at his wit's end, that's all. He doesn't know what to do about Peck."

"How hard is Peck trying to get you to move?"

"He sends his men here periodically."

"On raids?"

She nodded.

"Has anyone been hurt?"

"Oh, they don't hurt anyone. In fact, they're very careful not to. They knock down our tents, scare off our stock, scare the children—they scare everyone, actually. Then they ride away."

"And you regroup."

"Yes."

"Instead of just leaving."

"Yes."

"It would be easier to leave."

"No," she said emphatically, "it would not."

"This water isn't cold anymore," he said, "and I believe I can move my toes."

"Take it out and let's have a look."

He removed his foot from the water, and she gave him a towel with which to dry it. When that was done, she crouched down, lifted his foot, and rested it on her bent knee.

"The swelling is not so bad, but it will be a few days before you can put on a boot."

"If I had one."

"I'm sure we can find you a spare pair, until you can buy your own."

"Would it be all right if I stayed here until the foot is better?"

"You'll have to ask Andrew and the other men that. I don't have the authority—"

"But you have influence," Clint said. "If you wanted me to stay, Andrew would say yes, wouldn't he?"

She didn't answer.

"Wouldn't he, Iris?"

"Yes," she said, without looking at him. "I suppose he would."

He leaned forward and asked softly, "Would you put in a good word for me?"

Outside Andrew Ludlum stood around with some of the other men, talking about the stranger who had ridden into their midst.

"How do we know he don't work for Peck?" Lemuel Chapman asked.

"Shouldn't have let Iris cow you like that, Andrew," Sam Day said. "How you gonna get the gal to marry you if you don't show her who's boss?"

Instead of taking offense, Ludlum answered the question.

"She's a strong-willed woman, Sam. I don't want her to change. She'll come around."

"Forget about Iris," Chapman said. "What about this stranger?"

"Oh, he's no stranger, Lem," Sam Day said. "Leastways, we know who he is."

"We do?"

"Said his name was Clint Adams," Day said. "Don't you know who that is?"

Chapman looked around at the others, who were also staring at him.

"Am I the only one who don't know?"

Ludlum was about to say no, that he didn't know either, when suddenly it came to him.

"Wait a minute," he said. "Clint Adams? You don't mean that he's . . ."

"That's what I mean," Day said.

"He's who?" Chapman asked impatiently.

"I read books and stories about him back East, but I thought they were just legend."

Sam Day was one of the few in their number who had not come from the East.

"He may be a legend, but that don't keep him from being real."

"What goddamned legend?" Chapman demanded.

Day looked at him and said, "The Gunsmith."

Chapman's jaw dropped. Even he had heard of the Gunsmith.

"Jesus," he said in a whisper, "if he *is* working for Peck, we're in a lot of trouble."

"Yeah," Andrew Ludlum said, "but if he ain't workin' for Peck, and we can get him to work for us . . ."

The implications of that were lost on no one.

FIVE

"I'll get you some help," Iris said to Clint.

"Where will I stay?"

"I suspect with Andrew. He's the only one with a big enough tent, and no wife and kids."

"I wonder how he'll take to that."

"He's a decent man, Mr. Adams. He knows you need help, and he'll give it to you."

"And I'll thank him for it," Clint said, "if he doesn't shoot me first."

"Don't be ridiculous," she said. "Just wait here and I'll talk to him."

"Thanks."

Iris had only been gone a few moments when Olivia reappeared.

"Hi."

"Saw your mom leave, huh?"

"Yes."

She stood with her hands clasped behind her back. She was the picture of her mother, except her youthful skin was smooth and soft. Would she grow up to look like her mother, attractive but weathered? Or would she find some way to stay inside and become the beauty her mother could have been?

"Are you staying, Mr. Adams?"

"Yes, Livvy, I am. Can you keep a secret?"

"Oh, yes," she said, her eyes shining, "I keep wonderful secrets."

"Well, I think when your mother's not around and it's just you and me, you can call me Clint. Can you do that without her catching on?"

She frowned.

"It's . . . deceitful."

"Well, only a little."

"And wicked."

"Not at all."

She smiled.

"I'll do it . . . Clint."

"Good."

"And you can call me sweetheart?"

Clint studied the young girl for a moment, then decided against that.

"I think we'll stick to Livvy, okay?"

"Well . . . okay. Where are you gonna stay?"

"Your mom says I can stay with Andrew Ludlum."

"Oh?"

"Does that surprise you?"

"Well . . ."

"Do you think that because Andrew is in love

with your mom he won't want to help me?"

Her eyes widened.

"How did you know Andy loves Mom? He made me promise not to tell anyone!"

"I figured it out."

"You won't tell anyone, will you? He'll think it was me who told."

"I promise I won't tell anyone."

"Not Mom, either?"

Did she really think her mother didn't know?

"No, not your mom, either."

Livvy breathed a sigh of relief.

Outside the group of men saw Iris McCain coming.

"Here she comes, Lud," Sam Day said.

"Get ready to give her her way," Lem said.

"Why don't you boys take a walk, huh?" Andrew Ludlum said.

As Iris approached, the other men scattered.

"What scared them off?" she asked.

"You did."

"Me? They're afraid of me?"

"Well, sure. Didn't you know that?"

"That's silly, Andy."

"You think so, Iris?"

She looked up at him and asked, "Are you afraid of me, Andy?"

"Oh, me most of all, Iris," he replied. "How's our guest doin'?"

"He's going to have to stay off that foot for a few days, and he's going to need another pair of boots after that. Think you can help with any of that, Andy?"

"Well now, you know as well as I do that I'm the only one who has room for a guest, Iris."

"Will you put him up, Andy?"

"Sure, Iris, why not?"

Iris frowned. She hadn't expected Ludlum to agree so soon.

"What's going on?"

"What do you mean?" he asked.

"Why are you agreeing so readily?"

"Well, why not? The man needs help, don't he?"

"Don't try to pull the wool over my eyes, Andy Ludlum. What's going on?"

Ludlum lowered his voice and said, "Do you know who that man is, Iris?"

"He says his name's Clint Adams."

"But do you know who Clint Adams is?"

"No, but obviously you do."

"He's the Gunsmith."

"He's what?"

"The Gunsmith. You know, the famous gunman?"

SIX

Iris looked stricken.

"That man is a gunman?"

"Yes. Why so surprised?"

She shook her head, as if trying to dispel a fog from her brain.

"He . . . didn't seem the type."

"What type does he seem?"

"He's just so . . . sensitive."

"Really?"

"I find it hard to believe that he makes his living with a gun."

"Well, not only does he make his living with it, but he's the best there is."

Iris looked directly at Ludlum now.

"Is he actually here working for Peck, then?"

"I don't think so. I think he really was just passing through and hurt his ankle. Lucky for us."

"Why? Why is it lucky for us?"

"Because now maybe we can get him to work for us."

"Against Peck, and all his men?"

"That's right."

"One man?"

"Not just one man, Iris," Ludlum said, "this man, the Gunsmith."

"He would still be one gun against many—that is, unless you and the others were to back him up."

"Well . . . I sure as hell would. I don't know about the others. I can't speak for them."

"But you'd help him."

"That's right."

"Well, that's fine, then you and he would both be killed."

"Iris, listen—"

"You men and your guns."

"Peck's men are using guns, Iris. What would you suggest we use?"

"Words."

"I've tried to talk to him."

"Talk to him again."

"It wouldn't do any good. The man won't listen to words."

"Only force, huh?"

"That's right, Iris, only force."

"Andrew, you're such a gentle man. How can you condone this?"

Ludlum spread his hands in a gesture of total helplessness and said, "There's just no other way, Iris."

"Well then," she said tightly, "you had better go and talk to your hired gunman. He's not going to be much good, though, until his foot heals."

"And that'll be in a few days, you said," Ludlum said. "I think we can wait that long."

"Well, get some help and come and get him then. If he is a gunman as you say, I don't want him in my house—and Andrew, I don't want him near Olivia, do you understand?"

"I understand, Iris," Ludlum said, "but will he—or she?"

"Don't worry about her," Iris said, "I'll talk to her. You just make it plain to your hired gun—"

"He's not my hired gun yet, Iris."

"He will be," she replied, "if he's who you say he is, he soon will be."

SEVEN

When Iris reentered the house and saw Olivia, she gave Clint a quick disapproving look that he didn't quite understand. Did she think he had lured the girl back into the house?

"Olivia, come outside."

"Mom—"

"Come on!"

Olivia gave Clint a quick look and then stepped past her mother outside.

"I don't want you talking to my daughter, Mr. Adams," Iris said.

Clint was puzzled.

"Ma'am, I'm sorry, but . . . I don't understand. Have I done something?" Was she offended by their conversation, after all? He had thought they'd both held their own during their little debate. When she left the house, she hadn't appeared to be angry. He wondered what had happened to change her mind?

"It's not what you did, Mr. Adams," she said, "but who you are."

Oh! That he understood. Someone had recognized either him or his name and had told her of his reputation. He'd come to know her well enough during the short time since they'd met to know that she would definitely disapprove of that.

"Let me explain—"

"I'm sorry," Iris said, "I don't have the time. If you want to talk to someone, talk to Andrew. He is very impressed with your reputation."

She left the house and just a second later Andrew Ludlum entered.

"Mr. Adams."

"Ludlum."

Ludlum stood in the doorway for a moment, then stepped forward quickly and extended his hand.

"We didn't get introduced proper," he said. "Andy Ludlum. Some of the folks around here call me Lud."

"Hello, Lud. I'm Clint Adams."

"Oh, I know who you are, yes, sir, I do," Ludlum said. "One of the other men, he recognized you and reminded me."

"I see," Clint said, "and you told Mrs. McCain?"

"Uh, yeah, I did."

"That explains her disapproval."

"Oh, yeah," Ludlum said, shrugging, "I'm real sorry about that. Iris don't take much to guns, or gunmen."

"And she thinks I'm a gunman?"

Ludlum was confused by that.

"Uh, well, ain't you?"

"No, Andy, I'm not."

"But your reputation—"

"Having a reputation doesn't make something true," Clint said.

"But . . . you are good with a gun, ain't you?"

Clint couldn't lie about that.

"Yes, Andy, I am good with a gun."

Ludlum heaved a sigh of relief.

"Mrs. McCain said you'd be willing to put me up until my foot healed. Is that so?"

"Oh, sure, I'll be glad to make room in my tent for you."

"Well, I'll be much obliged for that. I'll need some help getting over there, though."

"You just sit there comfortable, and I'll get a couple of the fellas over here to help you."

"I'd like to check on my horse too."

"Don't blame you," Ludlum said, "that's a fine-looking animal."

"Yes, he is."

They stared at each other for a while, and Clint wondered if Ludlum was going to ask the question now or later.

"Well," the man said finally, "I'll go and get those boys to help. Be right back."

As Ludlum left the house, Clint wondered if he should just mount up and ride Duke out of there to Lordsburgh. In the short time he'd been there he'd managed to totally alienate Iris McCain, and any minute Andy Ludlum was going to try to hire out his gun. About the only one who didn't want anything from him was Livvy.

He decided to give it a day, maybe two. At that time he'd evaluate his condition, and the situation, and make a decision.

"Well?" Iris asked as Ludlum came out of the house.

"Well what?"

"Did you hire him?"

"Not yet."

"Did you ask him?"

"No."

"Why?"

"The time wasn't right, Iris," Ludlum said, slightly annoyed. "I'll know when the time is right, and then I'll ask him. I got to get some of the boys to help him over to my tent."

As Ludlum walked away, Olivia spoke.

"Ask him what, Momma? Hire him for what?"

"Never mind, child."

"Oh, Momma!"

The girl's exasperated tone attracted her mother's complete attention.

"What is it, Olivia?"

"When are you going to stop treating me like a child? I'm not a child anymore. Can't you see that?"

"Baby—"

"And I'm not a baby, either!"

With that Olivia stalked away from her mother, who stared helplessly after her.

EIGHT

"Is he gonna do it?" Lem Chapman asked.

"I didn't ask him."

"Well, when are you gonna ask him?" Sam Day asked.

"Later," Ludlum said, "after you boys help me get him to my tent. Come on."

He led them back to the house, and they followed him inside. Once there they stood around nervously.

"I'll need a hand standing up," Clint said.

The three men exchanged a glance, and then they all stepped forward and reached for him.

"I think I'll only need two of you, thanks. Just help me up and then support me between you."

"Yessir," Day said.

"We'll do that, Mr. Adams," Lem said.

As the two men assisted Clint to his feet, he

could have sworn they were trembling. Obviously, they all knew who he was now, and it made them nervous.

"I'll need my gun." He had taken it off and hung it on the back of a chair.

"I'll carry it," Ludlum said, picking up the gun belt and starting to sling it over his shoulder.

"That's all right," Clint said. "Just hand it to me. I'll carry it myself."

"Sure," Ludlum said, and gave it to him.

They helped him out of the house and, with Ludlum leading the way, walked slowly across the compound toward Andrew Ludlum's tent.

Word had spread by now who he was and that he was staying, and the rest of the people gathered to get a look at him. Clint didn't see the disapproving Iris McCain or her daughter anywhere. He felt as if he were on display and was starting to regret his decision to stay.

"My horse," he said.

"What?"

Sam Day stopped short and Lem Chapman took an extra step or two. This put Clint off balance between them and he almost fell. The two men held him fast and moved to get even on both sides of him.

"My horse," he said again. "I want to check on him."

The two men looked at Ludlum.

"Come on, take him over to his horse. Man's got a right to check on his own animal."

They changed direction and took him over to the makeshift corral where they kept their own stock. Among their sorry, swaybacked animals Duke stood out like a diamond in the rough.

They led Clint right up to the corral.

"Let go for a second," he said, and they did. He supported himself by leaning on the corral fence. "Come here, Big Boy."

Duke trotted over to where Clint stood. He looked the animal over for a few moments.

"How's he look?" Ludlum asked.

"Fine, he looks fine."

"We'll make sure he's looked after right and proper," Ludlum said, "won't we, boys?"

"Sure will," Day said.

"Durn right," Lem said.

"Want to go to the tent now, get some rest?" Ludlum asked.

"Yes," Clint said, "although I'd appreciate a drink before resting."

"Coffee?" Ludlum asked.

"Whiskey," Clint said.

"We got any whiskey in camp, Lem?" Ludlum asked.

The other man hesitated, then said, "I might have a bottle around somewheres."

"Good. We'll get Mr. Adams here over to my tent and then you go and fetch it."

When Lem didn't answer, Sam Day nudged him with his elbow.

"Okay, sure, why not?" Lem said.

"Andy, if we're going to share a tent, why don't you start calling me Clint?"

"Clint," Ludlum said. He beamed at the others and said, "I'm gonna call him Clint."

Clint frowned and then said to the others, "That goes for all of you."

"We can call you Clint?" Sam Day asked.

"That's right," he said, "you can call me Clint."

"Can we call you Gunsmith?" Lem asked.

Clint gave him a cold look and said, "No, you can't."

Lem blinked a couple of times and noticed the others looking at him.

"I was just askin'!"

"Well don't ask no more!" Ludlum hissed at him.

They walked Clint over to Ludlum's tent and helped him inside.

"I ain't got any beds, but we'll go and get your bedroll and bring it in."

"Good enough," Clint said, as they lowered him to the floor. He looked up at the two men and said, "Thanks for the help."

"Sure, Mist—I mean, Clint," Sam Day said.

Lem just nodded. He'd learned his lesson and was afraid to open his mouth. Both men left, leaving Clint in the tent with Andrew Ludlum.

"Andy, can I talk to you?"

"Sure, Clint."

"You've got to tell the others not to be afraid of me. My reputation, it's just stories, you know? Like a lie that grows bigger and bigger the more people tell it."

"Really?"

"Really."

"But—uh, I mean, you are good with a gun, though, right?"

"Yes, Andy," Clint said wearily, "I'm good with a gun, but take my word for it, that doesn't amount to very much in this world."

"I don't know," Ludlum said, "it's a hell of a lot more than I got."

NINE

Ludlum returned with Clint's bedroll just before Lem Chapman appeared with a half-empty bottle of whiskey. Moments later, probably following the scent of the whiskey, Sam Day appeared, and the four were together in the tent again.

"Crack that bottle, Lem," Sam Day said.

"I was savin' it."

"For what?" Ludlum asked.

Lem thought a few moments, then shrugged and said, "I don't know."

"Well, open it then. This is as good a time as any."

Clint didn't usually drink whiskey, but his ankle was throbbing and he was tired. He wanted to get some sleep and thought it might be easier with some whiskey. It seemed to him, though, that Lem

Chapman's half a bottle wasn't going to last long in the present company.

"Ain't got any glasses," Chapman said.

"Pass the bottle around, Lem. Let's get to drinkin'," Sam Day said.

"Clint first," Ludlum said.

Grudgingly Lem Chapman handed the bottle to Clint, who knew that things had gone too far now to change his mind. He removed the stopper, tipped the bottle up, and took a couple of big swallows. When Clint lowered the bottle, Lem was looking at him as if he had just taken a bite out of his firstborn.

Clint started to hand the bottle to Lem when Sam Day stepped up and snatched it.

"Me next."

Day tipped it up, and Ludlum had to grab it from him after three swallows.

"That's enough," he said. "It's got to go around." He started to take a swallow, then thought again and handed it to Lem. The bottle's owner took a few swallows, and then handed the bottle back to Ludlum with a swallow or two left in it. He watched sadly as the man lifted the bottle and drained it.

"That's it," Ludlum said, "it's gone."

"And so am I," Sam Day said, wiping his mouth on his sleeve. "I got work to do."

Day left and Lem stared after him.

"Sure, he leaves when the whiskey's gone."

"Don't you have some work to do too, Lem?" Ludlum asked.

"As a matter of fact, I do. See you later."

"Thanks for the whiskey, Lem."

"Yeah," Lem said sadly, "sure."

After Chapman left, Ludlum went over to his pallet and sat down on it. He had not offered it to Clint, for which Clint was grateful.

"You look exhausted," Ludlum said.

"I am," Clint said. "I could do with some sleep."

"There's something I wanted to talk to you about," Ludlum said, "but . . . I guess it could wait until after you've slept."

"I'd appreciate that."

Ludlum stared at Clint for a few moments, then put his hands on his knees and pushed himself to a standing position.

"Well, I'll leave you to sleep. Uh, a few hours then?"

"Probably," Clint said. "I don't know, maybe more."

"Okay, uh, I'll see you later."

As Ludlum headed for the tent flap, Clint said, "Hey, Andy?"

"Yeah?"

"Anybody around here play poker?"

Ludlum smiled.

"Sure, a few of us."

"You?"

"Every chance I get. You interested in a game?"

"Maybe later," Clint said, "just to pass the time."

"I'll fix it," Ludlum said. "See you later."

After Ludlum left, Clint lay down on his bedroll. He kept his gun close at hand. Now that everyone knew who he was, keeping the gun by his side was the wisest course of action.

Moments after he lowered his head, he was asleep.

TEN

When Clint woke up he was ravenous. He sat up, instantly aware of where he was. He looked down at his ankle. It was still swollen, but it didn't look as bad as it had. It still ached, though it didn't throb as much. He reached down to rub it and flinched from his own touch. It was still tender, and he knew he'd never be able to stand on it this soon.

From outside he could smell cooking, and it made his stomach growl loudly. As if he'd heard it, Andy Ludlum came into the tent at that moment.

"Ah, you're awake."

"How long did I sleep?"

"A little more than three hours." Ludlum sat on his pallet again.

"And the time?"

41

"A little after five. How do you feel?"

"Okay, except for my ankle and the fact that I'm hungry."

"Well, I can't help your ankle, but I can do something about you being hungry." He stood up and said, "Come on, let's eat."

Leaning on Ludlum, who was stronger than his frail frame indicated, Clint managed to walk outside, where the scent of food was even stronger. He saw that there were pots on two fires, with women tending to them. He looked around but didn't see Iris McCain or her daughter, Olivia. There was smoke coming from the little chimney on their house though.

"I'm gonna take you over to one of the fires so you can eat," Ludlum said.

"What about you? Did you eat already?"

"No, but I usually eat with Iris and Olivia."

"Oh, I see."

Ludlum walked Clint to one of the fires, where the woman tending the pot smiled at him. She was a chunky woman, probably in her late forties. Her smile revealed that she was missing several teeth.

"This is Wendy." It seemed an ironic name for the woman, who looked like anything but a Wendy. "She'll see that you have enough to eat."

Wendy nodded as Clint sat down on a hunk of tree trunk.

"What about that poker game?" Clint asked.

Ludlum smiled.

"I've got it set up. We can start anytime you want to."

"Later is good enough. I don't want to interfere with your, uh, evening with the ladies."

Ludlum frowned for a moment, then looked sheepish.

"Oh no, it's not like that."

"I didn't mean—"

"Iris and I are . . . good friends."

"Who are you kidding, Andy? You're in love with the woman."

Ludlum looked down at the ground.

"Does it show?"

"It shows," Clint said, "and I heard what some of the men said to you."

"She's a strong-willed woman."

"I found that out."

"Don't hold it against her," Ludlum said quickly. "She's a fine woman, Clint."

"I don't doubt it."

"She's a good mother to Olivia."

"A little hard, I think."

"Maybe," Ludlum said, "but she only wants what's best for Livvy."

"That's obvious."

"Andy!"

Ludlum turned and looked at Olivia, who was calling him from the door of the little house.

"I've got to go."

"Remember something, Andy."

"What?"

"A woman likes a man to be a man."

Ludlum stared at Clint for a few seconds with a frown, and then his face brightened.

"I think I know what you mean."

"Good. Enjoy your dinner."

"You too. See you for poker."

As Ludlum walked away toward the house, Olivia looked around him and waved to Clint, who waved back. Watching the man's progress, Clint was grateful that Ludlum hadn't attempted to broach the subject of hiring him. Maybe Ludlum had changed his mind about that.

His attention was diverted when Wendy offered him a bowl filled to capacity with a stew that looked and smelled delicious. He accepted it, and a fork, and when he looked back, Ludlum and Olivia were already out of sight in the house.

He turned his full attention to the stew, shoveling forkfuls into his mouth as fast as he could chew. He was half done before he slowed down enough to appreciate that it tasted as good as it smelled and looked.

ELEVEN

After dinner Olivia asked her mother if she could be excused. Ludlum was surprised when Iris said yes. She usually made Livvy stay and help with the clean-up chores.

"Will you help me clean up, Andy?"

"Uh, sure, Iris," Ludlum said. She had never asked him that before. Was she trying tonight to see what it would be like if they were married?

He thought it was strange, but stayed and helped with what he had always thought of as women's work.

"Where's Andy?" Clint asked.

Livvy had come out of the house after dinner and found Clint sitting in front of Andy Ludlum's tent. She sat down with him.

"He's staying to help Momma clean up."

"That sounds like something you should do."

She giggled.

"I usually do, but Momma told me she wanted Andy to help her tonight. She told me to ask to be excused after dinner."

"So she tricked him?"

Olivia giggled again.

"We both did."

"You look pretty proud of yourself."

"I am. Also, I got to come out here and talk to you. She told you not to talk to me, didn't she?"

"How do you know?"

"I know Momma. As soon as she found out who you were she didn't want me talking to you."

"Why not?"

"Oh, Momma's trying to keep me from growing up."

"It doesn't look like she's having any luck."

She blushed and asked, "Do you think I'm pretty?"

He was about to answer that yes, he did think she was pretty, but he suddenly realized that he might be asking for trouble. She was young enough to misunderstand his motives.

Luckily he was rescued by the appearance of Andy Ludlum, who had apparently finished doing dishes.

"Clint, are you ready for some poker?"

"Sure, Andy. Where are you going to set up?"

"Well, it would be easier for you if we played right here in my tent. The others will be here soon." Ludlum looked at Olivia and said, "Time for you to go, Livvy. We're gonna be busy."

"Playing poker?" she asked, pouting. "You call that busy?"

"Livvy!"

"I'm going, I'm going." She stood up and looked down at Clint. "Can we talk again, Clint?"

He looked at Ludlum, who shrugged and said, "I won't tell."

"Sure, Livvy," Clint said. "We'll talk."

As Olivia walked away, Ludlum said, "Looks like our Livvy has a crush on you, Clint."

"Just what I need," Clint said. "And what about you? I heard her mother had you doing dishes tonight?"

Ludlum shrugged again.

"What's the harm in doin' a few dishes?"

"Who's doin' dishes?" somebody asked from behind him.

Ludlum turned and saw Sam Day.

"Nobody. You got the cards?"

"Yeah."

"Where are the others?"

"Lem'll be along in a minute. Also Val Carson and Fred Carter."

"Six players," Ludlum said. "That's a game."

"Here comes Lem," Day said. "Let's get started."

TWELVE

The stakes of the game were small, but then Clint was only looking to pass the time and Ludlum and the others did not have that much money to play with. Consequently, two bits and four bits was the biggest the game got.

The others helped Clint into the tent, and then they formed a circle and played on the ground. Clint, being the better poker player by far, was the only winner. He took a combined fifty dollars from the other men, with Sam Day losing the most money, fourteen dollars.

"It's a good thing I ain't got a wife," he said as he was leaving. "She'd kill me."

Fred Carter did have a wife, and he said she would kill him for losing seven dollars.

Carter was the last to leave, postponing the inevitable. Ludlum collected the cards and sat on his pallet. Clint was already on his bedroll.

"You're a real good poker player," Ludlum said.
"When we play I usually win."

"I've played a time or two."

"Yeah, and for higher stakes, I'd wager."

"I was just trying to pass the time, Andy."

"I know that. Maybe I'll get some of my money
back tomorrow."

"Maybe."

Ludlum set the cards aside and glanced around
the tent nervously. Since it was Andy's tent and
he knew every inch of it, Clint could only guess
that Ludlum was trying to work up the nerve to
ask him something.

"Okay, Andy, come on."

"What?"

"You've been trying to ask me something all
day. Come out with it."

"It's that obvious, huh?"

"Yes, it is."

"Iris doesn't want me to ask you. In fact, that
was why she asked me to help with the dishes
tonight, so she could try to talk me out of it."

"I guess she didn't succeed."

"No," Ludlum said, "I got to ask anyway."

Clint reclined on his back with his hands clasped
behind his head.

"Okay, go ahead."

"We need your help, Clint. This is our home
now and we're trying to hold on to it."

"Why?"

"What?"

"Why are you trying to hold on to it so badly?

Is it because someone else wants it?"

"What kind of reason is that?" Ludlum was genuinely puzzled by the question.

Clint looked at him for a minute to see if he was sincere. What he saw on the man's face told him he was.

"That's just the way a lot of people are, Andy," he explained. "When someone else has something, they want it. Then when they get it, they discover they really didn't want it after all."

Ludlum pondered that for a moment and then said thoughtfully, "You know, I'm glad I'm not smart enough to understand that."

"Forget it. Tell me why you want this land so badly."

"A lot of us came out here together from the East to make homes for ourselves, Clint. The rest joined up with us along the way. We've all been looking for a long time, and when we got here we decided this would be it."

"It looks like good land," Clint admitted.

"It is. We all want to build our homes by this stream, some to grow crops, others to raise stock. All of us are tired of looking, though, and we don't want to leave."

"Then you'll have to fight for it."

"With what?"

"You had guns to point at me when I got here."

"And those are all the guns we have."

"Buy more."

"We don't have money for that. No, I'm afraid we can't put up much of a fight against Peck and his men."

"Then your other option is to negotiate with Peck."

"I have. I've talked to him until I was blue in the face—and black-and-blue in other places."

"He had you beaten?"

Ludlum nodded.

"More than once. Last time I went to town, he sent me back here tied to my horse. He wanted me to get here without falling off."

"Considerate of him. Well, it sounds like the only other way to go is to buy him out."

"And we don't even have the money for guns, let alone that."

"Then you're stuck without a solution."

"Well . . . we were until you showed up."

Clint sat up.

"I'm not your solution, Andy."

"You can be. Just work for us."

"Work for you? You just said you had no money."

"We can pay you fifty dollars, maybe even sixty."

"To do what?"

"I don't know . . . scare him, I guess."

"You want me to scare Peck and all his men?"

"Well, if his men knew you were here, they wouldn't want to go against you."

"They wouldn't have to," Clint said. "My gun is not for sale."

"Then don't use your gun. Just go and talk to him and make him think you'll use your gun. His men will believe you, once they find out who you are."

"They won't all believe me, Andy. At least one of them will want me to prove it."

"You can deal with one man."

Clint gave Ludlum a hard look.

"I won't kill a man for fifty dollars, or five hundred dollars."

Ludlum looked surprised.

"Five hundred! Did anybody ever pay somebody that much to kill somebody?"

Clint sighed and said, "It's been done."

"Hell," Ludlum said, "I'd kill someone for five hundred dollars."

Clint stared at the man for a few moments and then asked, "Have you ever killed a man, Andy?"

"Well . . . no."

"Do you think it's easy?"

"I . . . never thought about it before."

"Well, think about it now. Let's say I offer you five hundred dollars to kill Sam Day."

"Sam? I wouldn't do it."

"Why not?"

Ludlum frowned at him, as if it were a damned fool question.

"Sam's my friend."

"Five hundred dollars is five hundred dollars, Andy. You said you'd take five hundred to kill somebody."

"Not to kill a friend."

"Okay, so you'd take five hundred dollars to kill a stranger?"

"Well . . . if I don't know him, and I ain't mad at him, how could I kill him?"

"Andy, do you think someone is going to offer you money to go out and find someone you're mad at and then kill him?"

"Well . . . I suppose not."

"Then don't be making stupid remarks like that without thinking."

Ludlum hesitated, stung by Clint's tone, and then said lamely, "I'm sorry . . ."

"Go to sleep now."

"What about Peck and his men?"

Clint lay down on his bedroll with his back to Ludlum. He spoke after a moment.

"We'll figure something out in the morning."

"Hey, thanks, Clin—"

"Go to sleep, Andy!"

THIRTEEN

David Peck was finishing his cigar in his study when the girl arrived. Tonight it was Isobel, the dark-haired Mexican one. Actually, she said she was Spanish from Spain, and not Mexican, but the distinction was lost on a man like David Peck. To him if she had a Spanish accent it was a Mexican accent.

Peck needed to have a woman every night, and it was his foreman, Jeff Duel, who provided them. Usually, Duel got them from the whorehouse in Lordsburgh, like this one. Peck had told Duel long ago he didn't care who the woman was as long as she was attractive, skillful, and she wasn't the same one he'd had the previous night. Consequently he often got a girl he'd had before. Isobel, for instance, had been to the house three times before tonight, so this was her fourth visit.

Peck was a robust fifty, and part of Duel's standing orders about the girls was that they be under thirty-five. Isobel seemed to be right at the border. She was a full-bodied woman with long, inky black hair, and Peck knew from previous experience that the hair between her legs was just as dark.

She stood at the doorway to the study with her hands behind her back. The dress she wore was low-cut, revealing lots of pale cleavage.

Peck was surprised that he remembered her name. He didn't remember any of the others, so why this one? Perhaps it was because she had been here more than any of the others. That, however, was Duel's doing, not Peck's. Did the girl think he requested her? She should know that all he needed was a body, a pretty face, a wet mouth, and an equally wet place between a woman's legs. She should know that she was here to serve him in any way he saw fit.

He put his cigar in an ashtray, finished the port, and set the empty glass down on the desk next to the cigar, then turned to face the woman.

"Come here."

As she walked across the room, he felt himself growing hard. That was good. on occasion he'd had trouble getting hard, and it was always the woman who paid for it. David Peck never took the blame himself. It was always the woman who was not desirable or erotic enough to arouse him, and invariably the woman paid for it. Once—only once—his violence had gotten out of hand, but he had paid for that, giving Madame Sande enough money to satisfy her. After all, she did expect her girls to come back from his house in condition to continue working. Wouldn't he expect one of his men to come back in working order if he loaned him out?

Isobel stopped just in front of him and waited. She was trained well, this one.

"Kneel down."

She did so. Looking down at her now he became fully erect.

"Open my pants."

She did so. She knew enough to do only what he told her to do, nothing more—even though she knew what was to come next.

"Take it out."

She released his stiff penis.

"Stroke it."

She ran her fingertips over him, concentrating on the underside where he was the most sensitive. She stole a glance up at him and saw that his eyes were closed. Apparently tonight she was pleasing him.

"Now lick it," he said urgently, "suck it!"

She leaned forward and licked the head, then ran her tongue over the length of him. He was a large man, and she wetted him thoroughly before taking him fully into her mouth.

"Ah, yes . . ." he said, and she felt relief. If she managed to please him right from the start the night would go much more smoothly.

"Suck me to completion, girl, and then we'll go upstairs."

She closed her eyes and sucked him avidly. Her aim was to give him as much pleasure as she

possibly could, and she knew she was extreme-
ly good at what she did. Often, however, how
satisfied he was had less to do with the skill
of the woman and more to do with the mood of
the man.

Tonight he seemed in a good mood, and for that
she was grateful.

Later that night Isobel Vargas lay beside David
Peck in his bed and listened to his snoring. After
she had sucked him in his den, they had come
upstairs and he had instructed her to bring him
erect again. Luckily, using her pillowy breasts
and talented mouth she had been able to. He had
instructed her to get on her hands and knees then
and proceeded to take her from behind, grunting
and moaning until he climaxed once again, leaving finger mark bruises on her buttocks, hips, and
breasts.

Isobel fervently hoped that she had tired Peck
out enough so that he would sleep through the
night. If he woke up and wanted to have sex again
and was unable, she knew she would be blamed.
It had only happened with her once before, and he
had struck her, but it had happened other times
with some of the other girls. Her friend Anita,
red-haired and rangy, had been brought back one
night by Duel, battered, bruised, and unconscious.
Madame Sande had been paid enough to ease her
indignation at having one of her girls rendered
useless for several days, but Anita had received
no compensation at all for the beating she had
taken.

Isobel's thirty-sixth birthday was a full month away. She knew that Duel only took women who were thirty-five and under for his boss's pleasure.

Never before had she so looked forward to a birthday—not even as a child.

Peck woke the next morning and looked at the sleeping whore in bed next to him. He thought about waking her for a morning poke, but decided against it. They'd done it twice last night, and if he was unable to do it this morning—well, he wasn't in the mood to beat the girl today. It would, after all, be her fault.

Peck decided to get up and bathe. He'd send Duel up later to wake the girl and take her back to town.

In the bathtub he decided it was odd that he was being so magnanimous to the whore. He was, after all, not in good humor these days. The squatters were still on his land and were showing no signs of moving. He was thinking that maybe the raids he was sending his men on should have a more lasting effect than just scaring off their stock or pulling down their tents. Those kinds of scare tactics were obviously not working on these people. The raid he had scheduled for this morning would be the last of its kind. After this, more damage would have to be done—maybe even the permanent kind.

He'd have to talk to the sheriff first, though. If the man was not going to be reasonable about his tactics—well, the people of Lordsburgh would find themselves with a new sheriff, that was all.

FOURTEEN

Clint woke the next morning before Andy Ludlum. He sat up and reached down for his foot. He poked and prodded it just long enough to decide that the swelling had gone down considerably. Whether he could walk on it or not was another matter entirely—and then there were the boots.

He lay back down, put his hands behind his head, and stared at the top of the tent. If he could walk, he'd leave the camp today. Hell, if he could limp, maybe he'd mount up, ride to Lordsburgh, and get himself a new pair of boots. He'd been heading that way, anyhow, on his way to nowhere in particular.

He didn't want any part of these people's trouble, not when they were bringing it on themselves by being so stubborn. All they had to do was move on to another piece of land, one that nobody else wanted, and their problems would be solved. If they were too unreasonable to see that, there was nothing he could do about it.

For once he was going to mind his own business.

Several miles from the camp, thirteen of David Peck's men were getting ready to perform yet another raid on the squatters.

"This is a waste of time," Chris King complained.

"Doesn't matter," Jeff Duel said, "this is what the old man wants."

"But this ain't doin' any good," King said. "How many times have we scared off their stock and pulled down their tents? They round 'em up again, and they put the tents up again."

"I got to agree with Chris, Boss," Casey Dolan said. "We're wastin' a lot of time here. We should be doin' our own work. We got trees need cuttin'—"

"You should be doin' what Mr. Peck pays you to do," Duel said.

"Workin'," King said.

"Doin' what he tells you to do," Duel said, "or what I tell you to do. Any man who can't do that had better draw his pay right now."

Duel looked at each of the twelve men in turn. He was a big man in his early thirties who ran David Peck's crew with an iron hand. He was not above whipping up on a man to make a point.

Nine of the men with him at that moment had been hired to work on the trees; the other three had been hired later after the squatters had shown up. Those three were hired specifically for the raids, and the other men knew it. They didn't like having to take time off from their work to go on the raids.

"You got somethin' else to say, Chris?" Duel asked.

King scowled.

"Speak up."

"Do I get fired if I do?"

"No," Duel said, "you get fired if you refuse to do what I tell you to do, not for giving me your opinion."

"They were hired for these raids," King said, indicating the three men who had been hired for that purpose. "Why do we have to go along and help them? Ain't they gettin' paid enough?"

The three were Ray Brooks, Hank Dunn, and Rick Shelton, hard cases all. They'd been doing strong-arm and gun work for quite a few years, most often as a trio. They didn't particularly care if the other men came along or not. In fact, they agreed with King, and Brooks decided to say so.

"You know, Duel, the man's got a point. We were hired for this; we can do the job ourselves. We don't need your men to come along."

"They're amateurs," Hank Dunn added. "On one of these raids somethin's gonna go wrong."

"We don't want the blame when it does," Rick Shelton said.

Duel stared at the three men. He was often surprised at how they all seemed to be speaking parts of the same thought, or sentence.

"I'm gonna tell you three what I tell the others," he said firmly. "You get paid to do what I tell you to do. That's it, end of conversation. Everybody got it?"

Brooks, Dunn, and Shelton exchanged glances, then Brooks looked at Duel and said, "You're the boss."

"The rest of you?"

The nine other men nodded their assent, and Chris King said, "It was just my opinion."

"Good," Duel said, "now that I've heard it, I don't ever have to hear it again, right?"

"Yeah," King said, "right, Boss."

"Okay," Duel said, "get it done and we can all get back to work."

Brooks looked at the other men and said, "Let's go then."

Ray Brooks, Hank Dunn, and Rick Shelton never had a problem figuring out who was in charge. They alternated from job to job, and on this job it was Ray Brooks who was running things.

Brooks led the way toward the squatters' camp and held up his hand for them to stop when they reached a familiar rise.

"King!"

Chris King frowned and rode up beside Brooks. He could feel the presence of Dunn and Shelton right behind him.

"What ?"

Brooks looked at him.

"I agree with you."

"About what?"

"What you said back there."

"Yeah, well . . . thanks, but the boss don't agree."

"Well, we all know that we're wasting time doing things to these people that they can just as easily fix."

"That's what I been sayin'."

"What needs to be done is something more permanent," Brooks said.

King frowned.

"Like what?"

Brooks hesitated, made a show of looking at his two partners.

"We've been talkin' about this. We noticed the other times we've gone in there that a few of the squatters have guns."

"Oh yeah? I never noticed."

"Oh, yeah," Brooks said, nodding his head, "we saw a few pistols and a couple of rifles. We're lucky none of them are decent shots, but that don't mean they can't hit one of us by accident."

"That's right."

"And it won't be real fair if one of us gets killed while we're scaring off stock and tearing down tents."

"You got that right."

"So we just want you to know that we'll go along with you and the others—you know, if something has to be done?"

"Like what?"

Brooks wondered how a man could be so thick in the head. Maybe it was breathing all that sawdust.

"I mean, if one of them takes a shot at one of you. . . ."

"Oh, I get it," King said.

Good, Brooks thought. He and Dunn and Shelton had discussed this. They didn't mind doing a job when they were well paid, but every job had to come to an end. They'd been on this one for a couple of months, and they were getting bored. They actually did agree with Chris King that they were wasting their time. Now, if one of the squatters should end up dead—well, that might convince them to move when nothing else did.

"Tell the others, will you?" Brooks said. "We don't want any of us gettin' killed, do we?"

FIFTEEN

Clint sat straight up and looked around. Andy
Ludlum was still asleep. What time was it? What
had caught his attention? He held his breath and
listened, and he heard it plain as day.

Horses.

"Andy! Come on, Andy, get up!"

"Wha—" Ludlum turned on his pallet and
looked around the room, wild-eyed. "What the
hell—"

"Andy, wake up!"

"I'm awake! I'm awake! What is it?"

"Horses!"

"What?"

"Riders are coming!"

Clint struggled, tried to get his good foot under
him so he could stand. He staggered and came
down on his bad foot, which didn't want to hold

him. He gritted his teeth and got to his feet, albeit unsteadily.

"Andy, damn it, you've got to warn everyone."

"Shit," Ludlum said, getting to his feet. He was still bleary-eyed, but at least he was moving.

Clint had slept in his jeans, but Ludlum had stripped down to his long johns and was now looking around for his trousers.

"Forget the pants, Andy. Go!"

"Hell," Ludlum said, "we ain't gonna stop them anyway, Clint. They'll ride through and tear things down like they always do, and we'll put it back up."

By now the sound of the horses was so close that everyone had probably heard it anyway.

"Andy—"

"Okay, okay," Ludlum said. "Let me get my gun—"

"Forget the gun. Just get people out of their tents, or they might get hurt."

"All right! I'm goin'!"

He went out the tent flap, and Clint limped along behind him, strapping his gun on. He knew he was about to experience one of David Peck's raids firsthand, and he resented it. Why couldn't they have waited a day or two until he was gone?

Iris McCain was awake, getting breakfast ready, when she heard the horses.

"Oh no, not again."

Iris was convinced that one day one of these raids was going to result in someone getting hurt, or worse still, killed. She shivered, hoping that today would not be that day.

"Momma?"

She turned at the sound of her daughter's voice. Olivia was standing in the doorway of the room in which they both slept. She was still wearing her nightgown, and the frightened expression on her face made her look very young. At the same time Iris noticed for the first time that Olivia's body was now that of a young woman's and not a child. The flimsy nightgown she wore made that very evident.

"Are they coming back, Momma?"

"It sounds like it, honey."

"Why? Why do they keep coming back?"

Iris crossed the room and put her arms around her daughter.

"Let's just stay inside, Olivia. Maybe they won't—maybe they'll go away—maybe . . ." She stopped because even she did not believe her words.

From outside the sound of the horses came closer, and now she could hear men yelling.

She cringed when she heard the first shot.

SIXTEEN

Clint stood in front of the tent, balancing on his good foot. He didn't know if he was going to be able to just idly stand by and watch David Peck's men destroy the camp. As much as he wanted to mind his own business, he was here, and he doubted he'd be able to do that.

Andy Ludlum was going from tent to tent, and several men had come out by the time the riders came into view. Clint saw that there were easily a dozen of them, maybe more, and they had their guns drawn. They were screaming and yelling, like Comanches instead of white men, and riding down on the camp at full speed.

Lem Chapman came out of his tent carrying a rifle, and from the look on his face he was going to do something stupid with it.

"No!" Clint shouted, but it was too late.

Chapman raised the rifle to his shoulder and pulled the trigger.

Chris King couldn't believe it. Just as Brooks had predicted, someone had fired at them, and the bullet had come perilously close to him. He'd heard it whiz by his ear!

King pointed his gun at the man with the rifle and without giving him a chance to fire at him again shot the man in the chest.

Self-defense.

Who could blame him for that?

Ray Brooks couldn't believe that their plan had gone right so soon. One of the squatters had fired, and Chris King—primed to perfection—had fired back and killed the man.

He pointed his own gun at a man who was coming out of a tent, but before he could fire, something struck him in the chest.

That was when things started to go wrong.

Clint saw Lem Chapman fall, then saw Sam Day run toward him. He also saw the lead rider point his gun at Day, and he knew he could not stand by and watch another man be shot down.

He drew and fired in one swift motion, and the raider toppled off his horse.

Dunn and Shelton saw their partner fall from his horse and knew he'd been shot. That was it! All bets were off now.

They started shooting.

• • •

"Back, get back!" Clint was yelling as people came out of their tents.

Sam Day took a bullet; it spun him around and dumped him on the ground.

Clint fired again, and another man fell from his horse. There was no time to think about the consequences of his actions. He kept firing, taking two more men from their saddles, and suddenly they were turning.

Dunn couldn't believe his eyes. There was a man who seemed to be standing on one foot, and he was firing a gun with deadly accuracy. Already Brooks, as well as three of Peck's men, were on the ground, either dead or wounded. This was more than they'd bargained for.

He looked at Shelton, who silently concurred, and they turned their horses and started back the way they had come. Peck's men, seeing this, needed no further encouragement. They also turned tail and rode away.

Dunn and Shelton, however, had every intention of coming back. Brooks had been shot—probably killed—and that could not go unpunished.

Clint saw the men turn and ride off, but he ejected the spent shells from his gun and loaded new ones just in case.

"Jesus!"

He turned and saw Andy Ludlum looking at him.

"I never saw shootin' like that before!"

"Andy," Clint said, "see who's hurt. I think Lem Chapman might be dead."

"What?" Ludlum turned and looked around, saw his friend lying on the ground. Not far from him, Sam Day was sitting on the ground, holding his side.

"Jesus!" he said again.

"Yeah," Clint said grimly.

SEVENTEEN

Clint, Andy Ludlum, and Olivia McCain stood outside Sam Day's tent. Clint and Andy had carried Sam inside, and Iris had come over to look at his wound. The dead Lem Chapman had been laid out in his tent until they had time to bury him. Right now their concern was for the living.

Clint was standing with most of his weight on his good foot, but in all the excitement he had forgotten about the sprain. Once it was all over he realized how badly the ankle was throbbing, but he refused to give into it and remained on his feet. Little by little he was putting more weight on it. Soon he'd be able to limp around, but not without some pain. Small price to pay for getting his mobility back, though.

"I can't believe Lem's dead," Andy Ludlum said. "What happened? They never shot anyone before."

"Lem came out of his tent shooting," Clint said. "I saw him."

"Damn him," Ludlum said, shaking his head. "I told him that wasn't the way."

"Maybe he just got nervous," Clint said. "Maybe somebody on both sides got nervous. Sometimes that's all it takes to start a war."

"Is that what we have now?" Ludlum asked fearfully. "A war?"

"Maybe."

"That means Peck could come riding in here any minute with more men. They'd wipe us out."

"He'd have to explain that to the law," Clint said. "No, I think what he might do is go to the sheriff in Lordsburgh and tell him what happened."

"Why would he do that?"

"Because he'll make it sound like his men were the victims."

"Then what do we do?"

"I guess we should go into town and try to get to the sheriff first," Clint said. "Before we do that, though, I'm going to need a pair of boots. Can you find out if anyone in camp has a spare?"

Ludlum examined Clint's feet and then looked at his face.

"I hate to say this, but I think Lem's boots might fit you."

"A dead man's boots?"

Ludlum shrugged.

"What else are we gonna do with them except bury them with him? If you can use them . . ."

"What about his family? How are they going to feel about it?"

"He's got no family."

"All right, all right," Clint said. "Will you get them for me?"

Ludlum swallowed hard but then said, "Sure."

He left for Chapman's tent, leaving Olivia with Clint.

"Andy says you saved us."

"Does he?"

She nodded.

"He says you killed four men."

Clint didn't say anything.

"Did you?"

"I suppose I did."

"He says he never saw anything like it."

"Watching men die is nothing to see, Livvy. Your momma will tell you that."

"Momma can't be mad at you," she said. "Not for this."

At the moment Clint wasn't worried about whether Iris McCain was mad at him or not. Before he could say anything, though, Andy Ludlum returned carrying a pair of boots.

"Here."

Clint accepted the boots. He'd wear them until he got to town, and then he'd buy his own pair and get them off his feet—and he'd take a long, hot bath!

"Thanks."

The flap of Sam Day's tent was thrown back and Iris McCain stepped out. She had a stray strand of hair hanging down over her face, and her forehead was wet with perspiration.

"How is he?" Ludlum asked.

"He took a bullet in the side," she said. "I got the bullet out, and I've bandaged him. The rest is up to him and the Lord, I guess."

"If you've gotten the bullet and controlled the bleeding, he should be fine," Clint said.

She looked at him and said, "Oh yes, I forgot. You'd know all about bullet wounds, wouldn't you?"

"Getting them or treating them?"

"Both," she said, and then added, "and causing them, as well. I understand you killed quite a few men today."

"I suppose I did."

"How did it feel?" she asked. "Had you missed it?"

"Momma!"

"Wait a minute, Iris," Andy Ludlum said. "Clint only fired after Lem was shot. He probably saved Sam Day's life, as well as mine and a few others."

"You can't possibly hold that against him, Momma," Olivia said.

Iris looked at Ludlum and Olivia in turn and then at Clint.

"It seems you've got quite a few people on your side, Mr. Adams."

"We're not on his side, Iris," Ludlum said, "we're on the right side."

"There's nothing right about shooting people, Andy."

"Yes, there is, Momma."

"Olivia—"

"You're not being fair, Momma."

"Don't talk to me like that, Olivia."

"She happens to be right, Iris," Ludlum said.

"Look," Clint said, not wanting to cause an argument, "let's not discuss the pros and cons of killing people right now. Something has to be done."

"By you?" Iris asked.

"Iris," Clint said, "if you have any ideas, I'm sure everyone would like to hear them."

"As a matter of fact, I do."

"Fine," Clint said. "Andy, why don't you get everyone together so we can talk? Iris can have her say, and then you can have yours."

"Me?"

"Yes."

"That's just fine with me," Iris said. "Come along, Olivia."

"I want to stay, Momma."

Iris stared sternly at her daughter.

"Olivia—"

"Go with your mother, Olivia," Clint said.

"I don't need your help with my child, Mr. Adams!" Iris snapped. "Olivia—"

"I'll come along, Momma," Olivia said, and then added, "for now."

She started for the house ahead of her mother, who stared after her.

"She's not a child any longer, Iris," Ludlum said.

"What would you know about it?"

"You were married when you were her age," he said. "I know that much."

"Never mind me," Iris said. "My daughter is not going to make the same mistakes I did."

"Iris—" Ludlum started, but she turned and walked away.

Ludlum turned to Clint and said, "I'm gonna talk against Iris?"

"You're going to speak your mind, Andy."

"Against Iris?"

"You did it in defense of me," Clint said, "now how about in defense of yourself?"

EIGHTEEN

Jeff Duel couldn't believe what he was hearing. He was in the barn with Dunn and Shelton, and they had just told him that the raid that day had not gone quite as planned.

"Say it again, slowly," he said to Hank Dunn and Rick Shelton.

Dunn looked at Shelton and something silent passed between them that Duel didn't understand. It was Dunn who spoke.

"Brooks and three of your men are dead."

"How did that happen?"

"Somebody started shootin'."

"Who?"

"We're not sure," Dunn said. "One of your men—Chris King—fired a shot, but we're not sure if he was shot at first."

"You're telling me those squatters started shooting at you?"

"That's what it looks like."

"And King fired back?"

Dunn nodded.

"He killed a man."

"Then what?" Duel asked.

"Then he got killed, along with Ray and two other men of yours."

"Who the hell shot them? I thought those people didn't have guns."

"They had a couple, but all of their shootin' was done by one man."

"One man killed four and chased the rest of you off?" Duel asked in disbelief.

Shelton took up the conversation.

"Your men turned and ran," he said. "We followed, trying to get them back, but there was no stoppin' them. They were like thirsty cattle headin' toward the smell of water."

"And what about you two?" Duel asked. "Why didn't you go back?"

"We didn't know what we were dealing with anymore," Shelton said. "It looks like those squatters have hired themselves a gunman."

"And a damned good one too," Dunn chimed in. "He didn't miss a shot."

"A gunman, huh?" Duel rubbed his jaw. "We didn't expect that. For one thing, where would they get the money to hire someone as good as you say this man is?"

"That ain't our concern," Dunn said. "If you'll pay us off, we'll be on our way."

"Why are you leavin'?"

"We signed on to scare some squatters," Shelton said. "We ain't gettin' paid enough to go up against the man we seen in that camp today."

"No, sir," Dunn agreed.

"Just wait awhile," Duel said.

"For what?" Shelton asked.

"Let me talk to my boss. He might come up with more money, considerin' the way the situation has changed around."

"How much more?" Dunn asked.

"I don't know. I got to talk to him. I'll let you know."

"We'll need enough to bring in another man to replace Brooks."

"I'll tell Mr. Peck that."

"When are you gonna talk to him?" Dunn asked.

"Today—right away. I got to tell him all of this right away. Get yourself some grub and some rest, and we'll talk later."

Dunn and Shelton nodded and walked out of the barn, leaving Jeff Duel inside with his thoughts.

David Peck was not going to like this news one bit, and Duel didn't relish being the one who had to tell him.

NINETEEN

They gathered right outside Iris's house for the meeting to decide what to do. Clint still felt the best thing to do was to ride into town to see the sheriff. In fact, whatever they decided, he had no choice, because he had killed four men and that had to be explained. Whether or not someone from the camp went with him was their decision. So since he had no say in what they did, he stood off to one side. Olivia, since she was fifteen and had no say, stood with him. There were other, younger children in the camp, but they were unconcerned with the meeting and were off playing somewhere within earshot. The only other person who was not present was Sam Day, who was resting in his tent.

Iris was the first to speak, standing on her rickety porch to do it.

"I still feel there's more to be gained from talking than from gunplay."

"There's already been gunplay," a man shouted. "Lem Chapman's dead."

"I know that," Iris said, "but that was Lem's own fault."

"And four of Peck's men are dead," someone else called out.

"Yes, but none of us was responsible for that."

"Wait a minute," Ludlum spoke up. "We can't just throw Clint Adams to the wolves."

Iris gave him a hard look, and Clint wondered if Andy Ludlum would ever be a match for her—or be able to tame her.

"You will have your say, Andy, when I'm finished, remember?"

"Everybody else is yelling out," Ludlum complained. "Why can't I?"

"Yeah, let him talk!" someone shouted.

Others called out the same thing, including some of the women. Clint was afraid that people had already made up their minds about what should be done.

"All right, Andy," Iris said, obviously not happy.

"Clint could have stood by and watched Peck's men shoot up the camp, but he didn't. He saw Lem get killed, and Sam get shot, and he got involved before anyone else could get hurt or killed. We can't very well go to David Peck and say, 'Look we're sorry, but Clint Adams killed your men, not us.' How fair would that be?"

"Why should we take the blame for what he did?" a man asked.

"That's what I say," Iris said. "Someone should go and talk to Peck and make him understand that this was all a mistake."

"And who's gonna talk to him?" a voice asked. This time it was a woman. "You?"

Clint was surprised that a woman was apparently siding with Ludlum against Iris.

"Yeah," a second woman called, "are you gonna do our talkin' for us, Iris?"

Iris McCain looked confused. Clint knew that she had not expected popular opinion to be against her at all. That was the way people with lofty ideals were, they expected the masses to side with them simply because they thought they were the most civilized. She had just naturally assumed that most of the people in camp would be against guns, just as she was.

Clint knew she had a lot to learn about human nature.

Suddenly, Iris raised her chin.

"As a matter of fact, I will go and talk to Mr Peck. I'm sure he'll listen to reason."

"Don't be ridiculous, Iris," Andy Ludlum said.

"What?" Plainly, she could not believe her ears. "What did you say, Andy?"

"I said I ain't about to let you go riding into David Peck's arms. You'll get yourself killed."

"That's silly," Iris said naively. "He certainly wouldn't kill a woman."

Andy Ludlum looked over at Clint and asked, "What do you think?"

Clint had not wanted to get involved in the discussion, but now he'd been asked a direct question.

"I don't think you can depend on a man like Peck to do the right or civilized thing. Killing a woman has never been above men like him."

The others started to buzz, and Iris stood with her hands on her hips, looking out at them helplessly.

"On the other hand," Clint shouted, and then continued when the din had died down, "he might listen to reason if Mrs. McCain went to speak with him."

"Would you let her go?" Ludlum asked. "If she was your woman?"

"Andy Ludlum!" Iris was indignant. "I am not your woman!"

"Answer the question, Clint," Ludlum said. "Would you let her go?"

"No," Clint said, "I wouldn't."

With that Ludlum jumped up onto Iris's porch.

"I'm going into town with Clint Adams. He has to talk to the sheriff since he killed four men. With his reputation, he's gonna have to explain that."

Clint was impressed that Ludlum had surmised that.

Ludlum looked at Iris.

"After that," he said, speaking to the others but continuing to look at her, "I'll go and talk to Mr. Peck. Will that satisfy you, Iris?"

Instead of answering she turned on her heel and stalked into her house.

Guess not, Clint thought.

TWENTY

During the ride to Lordsburgh, Clint imagined
that Lem Chapman's boots were squeezing his
feet. He'd never worn a dead man's boots before
and he didn't like the sensation. Of course, he
knew it was his imagination, but they still felt
tight.

After the people had dispersed from the front of
Iris McCain's house—and she had gone inside
and slammed the door behind her—Andy Ludlum
had walked up to Clint Adams.

"You mind if I ride into town with you?"

"I don't mind at all, Andy."

"When?"

"Right now," Clint had said. "You got a saddle
horse?"

"No," Ludlum had said, "I'll just get the buckboard hitched up and take it in."

Clint had saddled Duke while Ludlum got his buckboard, and then they had headed toward Lordsburgh together.

"Those boots botherin' you?" Ludlum asked, looking over at Clint.

"Just feel a mite tight," Clint said. "My imagination, you know?"

"Can't say I do," Ludlum said. "I ain't got much of an imagination, and I ain't never wore a dead man's boots."

Clint didn't find comfort in either statement.

"Tell me about the sheriff of Lordsburgh," he said. "Have you met him?"

Ludlum nodded.

"I talked to him every time I got beat up by Peck's men."

"And how many times was that?"

Ludlum shrugged.

"Couple of times real bad," he said. "Once or twice not so bad."

"Where'd this happen?"

"In town."

"When was the last time?"

"Not for a while," Ludlum said, then added, "I ain't been to town in a while."

Clint had renewed respect for Ludlum for accompanying him into town now after what had happened to him on other occasions.

Jeff Duel could not think of the proper words to use, so he just told David Peck flat out what had happened.

"What do our men say?" Peck asked.

"They said it was Brooks and the others who started it, and then when Brooks got killed, Dunn and Shelton were the first to run."

Peck frowned.

"Do we know who to believe?"

"No."

"How many of our men were killed?"

"Nearest I can figure, three. Leastways, that's how many are missing."

"Any hotheads?"

Duel paused then said, "Chris King seemed kinda impatient. He said he was getting tired of just running raids."

Peck nodded.

"There's a good chance, then, that he started it, and the others are covering up because he was one of them."

"It's possible."

"Will Dunn and Shelton stay on now that Brooks is dead?"

"If we pay them enough money."

"How much is enough?"

"More than we were paying them before, plus enough to bring a third man in."

Peck sat quietly, looking down at the top of his desk.

"What do you want to do, Mr. Peck?" Duel asked.

Peck rubbed the side of his nose with his right forefinger.

"I'm not sure yet, Jeff. Keep them around, will you? Until I make up my mind?"

"Sure, I'll try."

"Have any of our men gone into town today?"

"Yes, sir, four of them, to pick up supplies."

"I think I'll go too. Maybe have a little talk with the sheriff."

"About what happened this morning?"

Peck stood up and said, "About a lot of things."

"Want me to come along?"

"No," Peck said, "I'll go myself. I'll come back with the other men. I'll see you later, Jeff."

"Yes, sir."

Duel started for the door, but Peck called out to him.

"Who's in town?"

"I'm not sure," Duel said. "Scott Bishop was going, and he took three others with him."

"Is Bishop a good man?"

"One of our best."

Peck nodded and said, "All right, thanks, Jeff."

Duel left the old man's office, wondering how the boss had been able to keep from getting angry about what had happened.

After Duel left, Peck sat back down. It seemed as if whoever had started the shooting that morning had been reading his mind. He'd just been thinking that it was time for some more forceful action, and this was it. Now all he had to do was deal with it—or maybe take it a step further.

TWENTY-ONE

"The sheriff's name is Lou Baker," Andy Ludlum said. "He's been sheriff of Lordsburgh for as long as we been here."

"What kind of a man is he?"

"If you ask me, he's a man in a job that he can't handle."

"So why does he have it?"

"Because David Peck wants him to have it. When Peck doesn't want him to be sheriff anymore, he won't be."

"Does Baker know that?"

"I don't know," Ludlum said. "I don't know him well enough."

"What did he do the times you were beaten up?"

"He told me he thought I shouldn't come to town anymore."

"That's it?"

"That's all."

"Doesn't sound like much of a lawman."

"In my opinion, he ain't," Ludlum said. "And if he's in Peck's pocket, I don't know what good talkin' to him is gonna do."

"He's still a lawman, Andy," Clint said. "He's got to go by the letter of the law or answer to the court."

"Or to Peck."

"Peck may control him, but he doesn't control the law. If we don't get any satisfaction, we can go to the law outside of this county."

"Peck'll probably buy that sheriff too."

"Then we'll go federal," Clint said. "Peck's money can't reach everywhere."

"I'd be glad of that," Ludlum said, "if you could prove it to me."

"Well, maybe I'll be able to."

When they reached the outskirts of Lordsburgh, Clint stopped to take a look at it before entering.

"Doesn't look like much," he said, surveying the collection of wooden shacks and buildings. There were three or four buildings of size, but the rest were hardly bigger than the house Iris and Olivia McCain were living in. Clint spotted a telegraph wire, though, and thought that kind of odd.

"It ain't," Ludlum said, "but it's all we got."

"So why do you want to stay in the area?"

"It's got a bank, a saloon, a general store, and a telegraph. That's all we need."

"Was the telegraph here when you got here?"

"Yes," Ludlum said. "The way I hear it, Peck paid to have it put in."

That figured, Clint thought.

"Okay," he said, "let's go in and do what we've got to do."

"I got to pick up some supplies too," Ludlum said.

"Fine, we'll go see the sheriff first, then stop for your supplies."

"Fair enough."

They rode into Lordsburgh.

As Clint and Ludlum rode into town, three men were standing on the porch in front of the saloon.

"Hey," one of them said. His name was Dick Parker. Everyone called him Dicky. "Ain't that a couple of the sodbusters the boss has been tryin' to get rid of?"

"Sure looks like one of 'em," Hal Gentry said.

"Don't recognize the other one," Ed Rivers said, "but the one on the buckboard looks like that feller Ludlum."

"Feller we beat up so many times already?" Gentry asked.

"By golly, that's him, all right," Dicky said. "Looks like he come back for more."

"We just the fellers can give it to him too," Gentry said.

"What about Bishop?" Rivers asked. "We're supposed to meet him here."

"We will," Dicky said, "just as soon as we finish with them two sodbusters."

• • •

Clint reined Duke in, and Ludlum halted the buckboard in front of the general store, which was one of the larger buildings in town. Right across the street was the sheriff's office, in one of the smaller buildings.

As Ludlum dropped down from the seat of the buckboard, he saw the three men coming across the street toward them.

"Uh-oh."

"What is it?"

"Three of Peck's men comin' this way."

Clint turned and saw the three men crossing the street together.

"Know any of them?"

"Maybe I do," Ludlum said, "I don't know. All the other times I run into his men I was coverin' my head so's I wouldn't get kicked."

"Just relax, Andy, and let me do the talking."

TWENTY-TWO

Andy Ludlum fidgeted from foot to foot while Clint Adams stood his ground as the three men continued to approach. They were all of a type, Clint noticed. Belligerent stares and swagger with little substance. The only question was whether or not he could avoid killing one of them. He already had enough trouble.

"What are you doin' in town, sodbuster?" one of them asked. "Didn't you have enough last time?"

"I ain't lookin' for trouble," Ludlum said. "I just come in for supplies."

"Is that so? You remember me?"

"Can't say as I do."

"You should," the man said. "You left here with my boot marks on your ribs last time."

"That was you?"

93

The man grinned.

"Me, Dicky Parker."

Clint stared at the man and asked quietly, "Dicky?"

Parker switched his gaze from Ludlum to Clint. "That's right, that's my name."

"That's a grown man's name?" Clint asked. "Dicky? Where'd you get a name like that?"

"What're you sayin'?" Parker asked. "You don't like my name?"

Clint stared into the man's eyes. He was the spokesman, therefore he was probably the leader. If he could take this man down first, the other two might back off.

"The name is fine, friend," Clint said, then added, "for a five-year-old, or a dog."

"Who you callin' a dog?"

"I didn't call you a dog," Clint told him. "I said you had a dog's name."

The man frowned, unsure of what the difference was, or if there even was a difference.

"You got a smart mouth, mister. Who are you, another sodbuster? This is the first time I seen you around."

Clint kept all of his weight on his uninjured foot.

"I've never seen you before either," Clint said, "and to tell you the truth, I don't ever want to see you again. Why don't you start walking?"

Dicky Parker stared at Clint, still looking puzzled, but then a smile spread over his face. He decided this was just another sodbuster to be stomped.

"You know what, sodbuster?" he said. "I'm gonna give you some of what your friend had last time, and then I'm gonna go to work on him again."

"I don't think so."

"No?"

"No."

"Why not?"

"Well, for one thing you don't have the brains God gave a rock, and for another, you're talking too much."

"I am, huh? What's that mean?"

"It means if you were going to do something you would have done it by now," Clint said. "It means you're all talk, so like I said, why don't you start walking?"

"Ooh, he told you, he did, Dicky," Hal Gentry said.

"Shut up, Hal."

"He really told you—"

"I said shut up, Hal!"

"Come on, Andy," Clint said, turning away from Dicky Parker.

"Don't turn your back on me, sodbuster!"

Clint knew that the man was perilously close to going for his gun. They had passed the point where administering a simple beating would satisfy him.

Clint turned back to face the man, still within arm's reach of him.

"You going to pull your gun, friend?" Clint asked. "If you are, you better do it now . . . come on, do it now . . ."

"Do it, Dicky," Ed Rivers said.

"Go on, Dicky, kill 'im," Gentry said. "He's askin' for it."

"You heard your friends, *Dicky*," Clint said, putting extra emphasis on the man's name. "Come ahead . . . come on, draw your gun . . . do it now— now, damn it!"

"Goddamn you!"

Dicky Parker went for his gun, but as he started to take it out of its holster Clint Adams reached over and put his hand over it. At the same time he drew his own gun and jammed the barrel beneath the other man's chin.

It got very quiet then as Parker's eyes went wide and he started to sweat. If possible, it got even quieter as Clint cocked back the hammer on his gun.

"Jesus, mister—"

"If I pull the trigger," Clint said, "the top of your head is going to heaven, while the rest of you goes to hell."

"Jesus—" Parker said again. "No, p-please—"

"If either of your friends draws his gun, you're a dead man."

"For Chrissake, keep your hands away from your guns!" Parker shouted.

"I gave you a chance to walk away Dicky, remember?"

"Y-yeah, I re-remember . . ."

"But you didn't take it."

"Mister, I'll walk away, now, I swear—"

"No, you won't," Clint said. "If I let you go now you'll try to think of a way to get even, and I'll have to kill you later, so I might as well kill you now."

Clint leaned in and pressed the gun even tighter to the man, as if he was preparing to pull the trigger.

TWENTY-THREE

"Clint," Andy Ludlum said, "you can't—"

"Shut up, Andy. This son of a bitch kicked your ribs in, remember?"

"It ain't worth killin' him over, Clint."

"You don't think so?"

"No."

"What do you think, Dicky? Do you agree with my friend here?"

"Yeah, yeah, I agree with him."

"Say it."

"Say wha—"

"Say it!" Clint jammed the barrel of the gun so hard beneath the man's chin that he knew the man would carry the circular imprint on his skin for some time to come.

"All right, all right," Dicky Parker said, closing his eyes. "I ain't worth it!"

"You know what, Dicky? I think you and my friend are right. I'm going to let you go."

"Jesus, thanks—"

"But do you know what this means?"

"N-no, what?"

"It means that my friend, here, just saved your life. He talked me out of killing you."

"Uh, yeah—"

"So you owe him your life. Do you understand that?"

"Sure, mister, sure, I understand—"

"Swear?"

"I swear."

"Say it."

"Jesus . . . he saved my life!"

"And what does that mean?"

"I owe him my life."

"So you'll stay away from him from now on, right?"

"Th-that's right, I'll s-stay away from him . . ."

"Good," Clint said, "very good. I'm going to lower my gun now, and holster it. If any of the three of you touches your gun, I'll kill all three of you."

"You that good, mister?" Hal Gentry asked.

"Hal, Jesus—"

Clint looked at Gentry and said, "Try me and find out."

He lowered the hammer on his gun and took it away from Parker's chin. As he holstered it, he kept a steady eye on all three men.

"Shit . . ." Parker said, rubbing under his chin.

"Your call . . . *Dicky*!" Clint said.

Parker stared at Clint for a few moments, then looked at Andy Ludlum.

"Thanks," he said, to the surprise of everyone.

"Forget it," Ludlum said.

Parker looked at the other two men and said, "Come on, we got to meet Bishop."

Parker led the way, followed by Ed Rivers and then—after a long look at Clint Adams—Hal Gentry.

"My God," Andy Ludlum said as the three men walked away, "y-you were going to kill that man, weren't you, Clint?"

"Not necessarily."

"Then you were just trying to scare him?"

"I was trying to make sure I didn't have to deal with all three of them."

"So to make sure of that you would have killed him if you had to?"

"Only if I had to, yes. I hate killing, Andy, but the secret to why I've lasted as long as I have is that I will if I have to."

"No hesitation?"

"In that situation?" Clint shook his head. "No hesitation."

"So how would you decide if you had to?"

"Andy," Clint said, turning to face the man, "that would have been up to him."

TWENTY-FOUR

They approached the sheriff's office, and Clint didn't bother to knock. The incident with Peck's men had him on edge, and he wasn't in the mood to be polite. Besides, he wanted to finish with the lawman and get himself a new pair of boots so he could take the dead man's boots off. He swore his feet were getting numb.

As they entered they saw the sheriff pouring himself a cup of coffee. He set the pot back down on the potbellied stove and turned to face them.

"Sheriff Baker?" Clint said.

The lawman pointed at Ludlum and said, "I know you, don't I?"

"Yeah, you do."

"Yeah, right," the sheriff said, "the sodbuster, got beat up a time or two."

"Right," Ludlum said, "by David Peck's men."

"Right, right. They're high-spirited, them boys who work for Peck. Thought I advised you not to come back to town."

"You did."

"Why are you here?"

"Sheriff," Clint broke in, "my name is Clint Adams."

Baker narrowed his eyes.

"I know that name, don't I?"

"You should," Andy Ludlum said, "he's—"

"Quiet, Andy."

But the sheriff didn't need Ludlum's help. The look on his face betrayed the fact that he finally recognized the name.

"The Gunsmith!"

"We need to talk, Sheriff."

"W-what about?"

The coffee cup in his hand was shaking, and some of the hot liquid spilled out onto his hand and wrist.

"Shit!" He hurriedly set the cup down on his desk and shook the coffee from his hand.

"Why don't you sit down and relax, Sheriff?" Clint suggested.

Baker wiped the rest of the coffee up with his shirtsleeve, then walked around behind his desk and sat down. He ignored the coffee cup now and stared at Clint. He knew his reputation and couldn't for the life of him imagine what the Gunsmith was doing in his office.

It scared the shit out of him.

"W-what can I do for you?"

"We've got to talk about what's happening to

these people out by the stream."

"The sodbusters?"

"This man and the rest, they're constantly being harassed by Peck's men."

"The way I understand it—"

"You understand it the way Peck tells you to understand it. That's the way I hear it."

"Uh, look, uh, Adams—"

"You could afford to look the other way, Sheriff, as long as nobody was getting hurt—"

"Well, that's true—"

"But that's changed now."

Baker opened his mouth to say something, then closed it when what Clint had said actually registered.

"What?"

"Some people got killed today, Sheriff."

"Who?"

"Five men."

Baker frowned.

"Who?" he asked again.

"A man named Lemuel Chapman, and four of David Peck's men."

Baker's eyebrows shot up.

"You killed four of Peck's men?"

"That's right," Clint said, "after they killed Mr. Chapman and shot a man named Sam Day. I wasn't going to stand around and wait to see how many more people they intended to kill."

"Four of Peck's men," Baker said, shaking his head. He was scared of Clint Adams, but he was also afraid of David Peck. Who, he wondered, should he be scared of the most?

"W-what do you want me to do about it?"

"Well, you're the law, aren't you?" Clint asked.

"Well . . . yeah . . ."

"I figure Peck's going to come riding in here to raise a big stink about his men being killed. Well, I'm here to tell you that they were killed in self-defense. They were pulling one of their raids and they decided to start killing people instead of just pulling down tents."

"Mr. Peck . . . wouldn't tell his men to do that."

"Are you sure of that?"

"I . . . well, yeah . . . I guess . . ."

At that moment the door opened and a white-haired man in his fifties entered. He was alone. He wore a black suit, boiled white shirt, and black string tie. He was not wearing a gun.

"Oh," he said, when he saw the three men, "sorry, Sheriff, I didn't know you were busy."

"Mr. Peck!" Baker stood up very quickly, almost knocking his chair over. "Uh, no, I'm not busy—I mean, these men were just telling me—uh, what happened today out by—"

"You're Ludlum, aren't you?" Peck asked, pointing at the man.

"That's right."

"And you—"

"My name's Clint Adams, Mr. Peck."

The name obviously registered with Peck immediately. Clint watched the man carefully and thought he could actually see him make a decision to take a different tack.

"Clint Adams," Peck said, nodding his head. "Well, I guess that would explain a lot of things."

TWENTY-FIVE

Across the street Scott Bishop approached Dicky Parker and the other men in the saloon, where they were standing at the bar. The first thing he noticed was that Parker was standing off by himself, away from the other two. The second thing he noticed was the look on Parker's face, which was even more sour than usual.

Minutes earlier Bishop had been over at Madam Sande's in one of the rooms with a red-haired woman named Anita. Of all of Madam Sande's girls, Anita was his favorite. She was tall and slender, with small but firm breasts. He loved the fact that the hair between her legs was the same flaming red as the hair on her head. He also loved the way she used her mouth on him, running it all over his body, finding places to put it that he didn't even know existed. Bishop was twenty-eight, and he'd been with women before, but none like Anita Connors.

Before letting him leave her room, she had pinned him to the door and, using her mouth, brought him to fullness when he thought he was all done. She took his penis fully into her mouth then and sucked him until he exploded.

Bishop walked over to the other two men and ordered a beer. His legs were still shaky from Anita's mouth.

"What's wrong with him?" he asked, nodding toward Parker.

"He's embarrassed," Hal Gentry said.

"About what?"

"Some sodbuster got the drop on him and made him eat dirt."

Bishop sipped his beer.

"What sodbuster?"

"You know, from that group out by the stream? That fella got worked over three or four times?"

"Him? I thought he learned his lesson. He made Parker eat dirt?"

"No, the fella who was with him. He baited Parker, and when Dicky went for his gun this fella pinned it to the holster. He put his gun under Dicky's chin, and I never even saw him draw it."

"Me neither," Rivers said. "Fella must be fast!"

"That so?"

Scott Bishop considered himself quite a hand with a gun, and this news interested him.

"What's this sodbuster's name?"

"Don't know," Gentry said.

"Didn't you know him?"

"Never saw him before," Rivers said.

Bishop stroked his jaw.

"I wonder if those sodbusters went and hired themselves a gun."

Over in the sheriff's office Clint Adams and David Peck looked each other over.

"What does it explain?" Clint asked.

"Well, for one thing it explains how you managed to kill four of my men."

"They were trying to shoot unarmed people."

"That's not the way I heard the story."

"That's the way it was."

"I can't believe everyone was unarmed in that camp but you."

"No, there were a few other guns, but it didn't seem to matter to your men who had guns and who didn't."

"Really. I'll have to look into that. I was actually coming in to swear out a complaint against those people, but it seems my complaint should be against you."

"I've already made my report to the sheriff," Clint said. "You're welcome to make yours."

"Thanks, I will."

Clint turned and pointed a finger at the lawman.

"If you don't go according to the letter of the law, Sheriff, I'm afraid I'm going to have to take this to a federal marshal."

"Oh, I don't think that will be necessary, Mr. Adams," Peck said. "As a matter of fact, why don't you come by my house later this evening and we can talk it over."

"Talk what over, Mr. Peck? This incident? Why don't we talk about the whole thing?"

"The whole thing? I'm afraid I don't understand. To what whole thing—oh, I see. Are you taking it upon yourself to represent these . . . these squatters?"

"They're just looking to make a home for themselves, Mr. Peck."

"On my land."

"As I understand it, you have no legal right to that land."

"*Yet*, Mr. Adams," Peck said, "the operative word here is yet."

"Well, until you do, I don't see how you can expect to push them off—uh, legally, that is."

Peck looked at the sheriff, and then at Ludlum, who he hadn't spoken to again since the first time.

"This is not the right place to discuss this," he said then. "I will repeat my invitation, sir. Come to my house, perhaps even for dinner, and we will discuss . . . everything."

Clint stared at Peck for a few moments and then nodded his head.

"All right, Mr. Peck, I accept your invitation. I'll be there."

"Good. Around seven?"

"Fine."

"Now, I think I will make my report to the sheriff—that is, if you are finished with him?"

Clint turned and looked at the lawman, for whom he had very little respect.

"Yes, I'm finished with him."

• • •

Outside, in front of the office, Andy Ludlum said, "Are you actually gonna have dinner with him at his house?"

"Sure, why not?"

"I can't believe this," Ludlum said. "What if he tries to kill you?"

"Right in his house? I don't think so, Andy. I think he really wants to talk."

"I still think it's dangerous," Ludlum said. "I think I should go with you."

Clint put his forefinger against Ludlum's chest and said, "You, my friend, weren't invited."

"He's gonna offer you money."

"Maybe."

"That's how men like him work."

"So? Are you afraid I'm going to take it? Is that what this is about?"

Ludlum didn't answer.

"We'll just have to see what happens, Andy," Clint said. "We'll just have to wait and see."

TWENTY-SIX

They agreed not to discuss it anymore.

"Why don't you go and get your supplies?" Clint suggested.

"What are you gonna do?"

"I'm going to go and buy a pair of new boots and get these off my feet." Clint looked down at his feet in distaste. "You can bury these next to Chapman's grave. Maybe then I'll be able to feel my feet again."

"And after that?" Ludlum asked. "I mean, after you get your new boots?"

"Andy," he said, "after that I'm going to get a room at the hotel."

"You ain't comin' back to camp?"

"No."

"Why not?"

"There's no reason to, really," Clint said. "I can

be more comfortable here, and you won't have to be cramped in your tent."

Ludlum was giving Clint a suspicious look.

"Andy, I can't make you believe that I'm not going to let David Peck hire me. You're just going to have to take my word for it. I haven't given you any reasons to disbelieve me up to now, have I?"

"No, you ain't."

"So?"

Ludlum looked down at the ground sheepishly.

"I guess I'm just the suspicious type."

"There's nothing wrong with that, Andy," Clint said. "Sometimes it keeps you alive. You've got to know, though, when to control it."

"Like now?"

"Like now."

"Olivia's not gonna like this, you know."

"I know," Clint said, "but Iris will love it. Go and get your supplies, and I'll meet you at the general store when I'm done."

"You're gonna have to come with me," Ludlum said.

"Why?"

"Because that's the only place in town that sells boots."

Clint shook his head.

"Now you tell me."

TWENTY-SEVEN

"What the hell did you tell him?" Peck demanded of Baker when Clint and Ludlum had left the office.

"I didn't tell him anything," Baker said. "Do you know who that was?"

"Yes, I know."

"That was the goddamn Gunsmith, that's who it was. He'd kill you just as soon as look at you, that's what they say about him."

"I said I know who it was, Baker. Don't worry about Mr. Adams, I'll be taking care of him one way or another."

"Is what they said true?" Baker said. "Somebody was killed today?"

"Four of my men," Peck said, shaking his head. "I can't help but be impressed with that. One man killed four. Amazing."

"Well, he's the Gunsmith—"

"Stop saying that! What are you going to do about it . . . Sheriff?"

"What can I do? Arrest him? He says it was self-defense. Arrest your men? You'd never let me do that . . . would you?"

"No, you goddamned fool, I wouldn't."

"So what am I supposed to do?"

"Nothing," Peck said, "not a thing—which is what you do very well, isn't it?"

"Mr. Peck—"

"Just stay out of the way, Baker, and you'll do fine. Understand?"

"Mr. Peck—"

"Do you understand?"

Baker backed off.

"Yes, sir, I understand."

"Good. Now stay in your office for the next hour or so."

"Why?"

Peck looked at the man like he was crazy.

"Because I just told you to!"

Baker looked away.

"All right."

"I've got four men in town. Do you have any idea where they are?"

"No, I—"

"Jesus, what am I asking you for? Just stay put, all right?"

"Yes."

Peck turned and left the office. Looking across the street, he saw Clint Adams and Andrew Ludlum going into the general store. Further

down the street was the saloon, and where else
would he expect his men to be?

Scott Bishop was the first one to spot David
Peck as he entered the saloon, and he nudged
Hal Gentry.

"Mr. Peck," Bishop called out.

Peck approached them.

"You're Bishop, right?"

"That's right, sir."

"Bring your beer over here, Bishop," Peck said,
"and bring me one too."

"Yes, sir."

Peck turned and surveyed the saloon. It was
still early and aside from his four men at the
bar there were only two other men in the place,
sitting at separate tables. He chose a table in the
corner and walked to it. Moments later Bishop
joined him with two beers.

"You didn't get these mugs confused, did you?"
he asked Bishop as the man set the beers down.

"No, sir," Bishop said, "this one's mine."

Peck eyed his mug dubiously. It was bad enough
he had to drink out of glasses other people
had used—goddamn bartenders hardly cleaned
them—he didn't want to drink out of one Bishop
had just had his mouth on. He decided not to drink
the beer at all.

"Sit down."

"Yes, sir."

"There was an incident this morning that I want
you to be aware of . . ." Peck said, and he went on
to tell Bishop what had happened that morning.

"Four men?" Bishop said. "Killed by one?"

"Not just any man, though, Bishop," Peck said. "It was Clint Adams."

Bishop sat back in his chair and whistled.

"You know who he is?"

"Sure," Bishop said, "the Gunsmith."

"That's right, the Gunsmith."

"There's somethin' you should know, sir."

"What?"

Bishop told Peck about the incident between the man he now assumed was Clint Adams and Dicky Parker.

"What the hell was Parker thinking? Who told him—never mind. Which one is he?"

"The one standing alone at the bar."

"Get him over here."

"Yes, sir."

Bishop walked over, spoke to Parker, and then brought him over.

"You wanted to see me, Mr. Peck?" Parker asked.

"You're Dicky Parker?"

"That's right."

"You're fired, Parker. Collect your wages and your belongings and get off my land."

TWENTY-EIGHT

"What?" Dicky Parker's eyes popped, and even Scott Bishop looked surprised.

"You heard me. You're goddamned fired!"

"B-but why?"

"I don't like having cowards working for me."

"Now wait a minute," Parker said, drawing himself up. "Who says I'm a coward?"

"Did you have a run-in this morning where a man backed you down?"

"That—that wasn't—that was—"

"That was Clint Adams who backed you down, Parker," Peck said. "Did you know that?"

"Clint—you mean . . . the Gunsmith?" Parker paled.

Peck nodded.

"That's who I mean."

"Jesus—"

"Are you afraid of him?"

"Well . . . no, I mean, well, he is the Gun-smith—"

"You want your job back?"

"Yes, sir."

Peck looked at Bishop, considered sending the man away, then decided to let him hear what he had to say.

"There's only one way."

"What's that, sir?"

"I don't want Clint Adams leaving this town alive," Peck said. "Do you think you can handle that?"

Parker swallowed.

"You want me to face him—"

"I don't care if you face him or shoot him in the back," Peck said. "I just want him dead. Under-stand?"

"Well . . . yes, sir, but—"

"But what? You want your job back, don't you?"

"Well, yes, sir, but I ain't never hired out to kill a man before—"

"Don't worry, Parker," Peck said, "you'll be paid accordingly."

"Well . . . what if I use help?"

"Your friends at the bar?" Peck asked, looking past him.

"Yes, sir."

"They'll be rewarded too. Can you take care of this for me . . . Dicky?"

Parker stood up straight as Peck used his first name and said, "Yes, sir, you can count on me."

TWENTY-NINE

After Dicky Parker went back to the bar to talk
to Gentry and Rivers, Peck told Scott Bishop to
sit back down and finish his beer.

"Mr. Peck, with all due respect, those boys are
not gunmen."

"That's why I said I don't care how it's done,
Bishop. They can shoot a man in the back just as
well as anyone else."

"Mr. Peck, if you really want Clint Adams killed,
I'm pretty good with a gun."

"Are you good enough to take the Gunsmith,
Bishop?" Peck asked.

"Well, he's not as young as he used to be, Mr.
Peck, and reputations do tend to be blown up."

"That doesn't answer my question."

"I don't know if I can take him, sir, but I'm
willing to try."

Peck shook his head.

"That's not good enough, son. I need to be sure, and back-shooting is surer than letting you go up against him. Do you want to be in on this bonus—"

Bishop shook his head firmly.

"Back-shooting is not my style, Mr. Peck—no offense meant."

"None taken. I would like you to do something for me, though."

"What?"

"Stay in town and observe. Let me know what happens. Come back as soon as Adams is dead and tell me. You can do that, can't you?"

Bishop had the feeling that he had lost Peck's respect—or any chance for it—when he refused to back-shoot Clint Adams.

"I can do that, sir."

"Good, good. I'll be counting on you. I'm going back to my house now. I look forward to hearing from you later."

Bishop watched Peck leave the saloon, then looked at the man's untouched mug of beer.

Clint was not at all choosy about boots. The point was to get the dead Lem Chapman's boots off his feet. He simply picked out the first pair he saw in his size and bought them. He removed Chapman's boots right in the store and donned the new ones. That done, he wasn't quite sure what to do with the old ones, discard them or give them back to Andy Ludlum.

Ludlum was at the counter settling up for the

supplies he had bought—or trying to.

"I can't carry you and your friends much longer, Mr. Ludlum," the clerk said. "I'm going to need at least something to put down on your account."

"I know, Mr. Hobbs. We're real grateful that you've stayed with us this long. We really need these supplies—"

Ludlum started to pick up what was on the counter, but Hobbs put his hand on top of the stack of articles and held them down firmly. He was a big, beefy man, and Ludlum had no chance against his strength.

"I need something, Mr. Ludlum, even if it's just a few dollars."

From behind, Clint saw Ludlum's shoulders slump.

"Christ," he said to himself and approached the counter.

"Here," he said to the clerk, handing him ten dollars, "is this enough?"

"You already paid for the boots, sir," the man said, somewhat confused.

"No, this is to put down on Mr. Ludlum's account. Is it enough for you to let him have these supplies?"

The man took the ten dollars and said, "More than enough, sir. Thank you."

"We'll get you the rest as soon as we can, Mr. Hobbs," Ludlum promised.

Hobbs removed his hand from the supplies, and Clint helped Ludlum carry them out to the buckboard.

"We're in your debt even further, Clint," Ludlum said. "We'll pay you back—"

"We're even, Andy," Clint said. "You took me in when I was hurt, gave me a place to stay."

"How is your ankle, by the way?"

"Well, with the new boots I'm finding out why the old ones felt tight. My ankle is still a little swollen."

"Then it wasn't Lem's ghost squeezing your feet?"

Clint laughed.

"No, I guess it wasn't. By the way, what do you want to do with Chapman's boots?"

"He's buried already," Ludlum said. "Why don't you just throw them away?"

Clint nodded and looked around for a place to toss them. Instead he saw an old man sitting in the street, one elbow resting on the boardwalk. He looked homeless, probably the town drunk. His clothes were tattered and torn, his hands, face, and neck were caked with filth. He looked like he could use a pair of boots—and a bath.

Clint walked over and looked down at him.

"I need a drink," the old man said, looking up at Clint.

"Here you go, old-timer," Clint said. He gave the man four bits, then handed him the boots.

"New boots!" the old-timer said, although they were hardly new.

"Get a drink and a bath to go with them, friend," Clint suggested.

"Thanks, mister!"

Clint walked back to the buckboard and noticed Ludlum looking at him strangely.

"That was a kind act, Clint," Ludlum said.

"I guess so," Clint said, feeling vaguely embarrassed. "How about a drink before we go back?"

Worriedly, Ludlum looked over at the saloon. Clint knew what he was thinking.

"I don't know, Clint." Ludlum turned his head and looked at him again. "What if Peck's men are still around?"

"I'm sure not looking for trouble, Andy, but I am thirsty. What do you say?"

Ludlum thought a moment, then said, "Well, I am thirsty."

"All right then," Clint said. "Let's go."

THIRTY

Peck was gone by the time Clint and Ludlum entered the saloon. Dicky Parker, Hal Gentry, and Ed Rivers, though, were still at the bar. Moments before Clint and Ludlum entered, they were still discussing Peck's proposition.

"How much of a bonus?" Gentry wanted to know.

"I didn't ask," Parker said, "but we all know how rich Peck is. It's bound to be a lot."

"I didn't hire on with him to kill nobody," Ed Rivers said.

"Hey," Parker said, "he made a fool out of me on the street."

"That was you," Rivers said, "not me."

"It could have been you, Ed," Parker said. "Tell me you woulda done different, huh?"

123

Rivers didn't answer.

"He'll probably pay us enough money so's we can move on, not have to work for a while," Parker said. "How does that sound?"

"Sounds good to me," Gentry said.

"Ed?"

Rivers still didn't answer.

"Ed," Parker said, "when we make our move, you better back us up."

"What do you need to shoot a man in the back?" Rivers wanted to know.

Before Parker could answer, though, the batwing doors opened and the subject of their conversation walked in.

"What about the other one?" Gentry asked urgently.

"Forget him," Dicky Parker said. "He ain't armed. This is our chance, Hal. We wait for him to have his drink and leave."

Gentry nodded, and then they fell silent and paid attention to their beers.

Still seated in the corner, Scott Bishop saw Clint Adams enter with the other man. He knew that Dicky Parker would not pass up a chance to get even with Adams, especially when he was getting paid for it.

Bishop would have liked to try his hand against Adams. He was getting tired of the kind of work he was doing for Peck. He was not a lumberman, and killing Adams would be his way out. He could leave Lordsburgh with Clint Adams's reputation, and probably some bonus money from Peck.

But that wouldn't happen if Parker and his friends shot the man in the back.

THIRTY-ONE

When Clint and Ludlum entered the saloon, they saw Dicky Parker and the other two men standing at the far end of the bar. There were three other men in the place, sitting at three different tables, but none of them seemed connected in any way to the three at the bar. Keeping an eye on them, Clint and Ludlum walked to the other end, near the window.

"Beer," Clint said, "two of them."

"Comin' up."

The bartender had been at his job long enough to know when there was tension in the air.

He drew the beers and set the mugs down in front of them, then got as far away from them as he could. Ludlum followed him with his eyes, then looked at Clint.

"He acts like we got the plague or somethin'," he said to Clint.

"Forget it," Clint said. "He probably heard a conversation that was going on before we got here. He's expecting trouble."

"Aren't you?"

Clint sipped his beer and said, "No."

Actually, he had hoped that Peck's three men would be gone when they came into the saloon. He wasn't looking for trouble, and he truly had wanted a beer very badly. He hoped that the beer would not turn out to be a lot more expensive than it should.

He risked a look down the bar at Dicky Parker and his friends. There was no one standing between him and Parker, but the man seemed very interested in his beer.

"Aren't you gonna drink your beer?"

He looked at Ludlum, and then at the man's mug, which was empty.

"Not as fast as you drank yours," Clint said. "Want another?"

"No," Ludlum said, "no, I'll just wait for you to finish yours."

Dicky Parker kept his head down, but out of the corner of his eye he watched Clint Adams in the mirror behind the bar. He was waiting for his chance. As soon as Adams turned to leave the saloon, presenting him with his back, he'd make his play. Whether or not Gentry and Rivers backed him up didn't concern him anymore. How hard could it be to shoot a man in the back?

After all, it had been done to Wild Bill Hickok, right?

Scott Bishop sat back in his chair and watched what was starting to happen in front of him. He knew that Dicky Parker would make a move as soon as he had Clint Adams's back. A man like Clint Adams deserved more than being shot in the back in a dirty saloon.

What Bishop didn't know was what he was going to do when it started to happen.

"Clint," Ludlum said nervously.

Parker was still staring down into his beer—or seemed to be. He was apparently intent on making Clint believe he wasn't interested in him. In Clint's experience that meant one of two things. The man was either afraid to look at him, or he was planning something underhanded.

"Clint."

He looked at Ludlum, who was growing more nervous by the minute. He decided to put the man out of his misery.

Clint drained his beer, set the mug down on the table, and said, "All right, Andy. Let's go."

It was happening.

Dicky Parker saw Clint Adams turn in his direction and then keep on going until he was walking toward the door. His back looked as big and broad as the side of a barn, and Parker imagined he could see a bull's-eye painted on it.

He turned to his left, took one step away from the bar, and drew his gun.

Hal Gentry had not been watching Clint Adams. Instead, he kept his eyes on Dicky Parker, waiting for the man to make his move. When Parker took one step away from the bar, Gentry took two, turned, and reached for his gun.

Right up until the last moment Ed Rivers had been unsure of what he was going to do. While he didn't approve of shooting Clint Adams in the back, he knew he could use the money that David Peck was going to pay him.

He didn't like it, but he took three steps back from the bar, turned, and put his hand on his gun.

Scott Bishop watched the action unfolding in front of him and knew he couldn't let it happen. Clint Adams deserved to die face-to-face, not shot in the back by three cowards.

He tensed, and moved.

Andy Ludlum turned to follow Clint Adams out of the bar. As he did, he saw the three men at the far end of the bar start to move, and he knew immediately what was happening.

"No!" he shouted.

He threw himself at Clint Adams, putting himself between Clint and the three men. He put his hands on Clint's back and pushed just as he heard a shot and felt a burning pain in his own back.

• • •

Clint heard Ludlum's cry, felt the push, and heard the shot. It was not a shot that was unexpected. In fact, he had decided that Parker was going to try something, and he was ready. Andy Ludlum's shove put him off balance, and for his unnecessary good deed, the man had gotten himself shot.

THIRTY-TWO

Scott Bishop stood up so quickly he knocked his chair over. At the same time he used his left hand to toss the table out of the way. With his right he drew his gun and fired twice, both shots hitting home. The first struck Ed Rivers even before he could remove his gun; the second hit Hal Gentry just as he was about to fire. Both men staggered and fell, Gentry actually falling against Parker.

Bishop didn't fire a third time.

Clint regained his balance and turned, hearing two shots as he did. He was surprised that he wasn't hit. He glanced quickly at Andy Ludlum, but there was no time to check on him. Instead, he looked at the bar where the three men had been standing, but only one was now. The other two were falling. Someone else had fired, not them.

Dicky Parker stood in shock. The sound of the two shots stunned him, and then he felt Gentry fall against him. He turned and watched his companions tumble. When he turned back toward Clint Adams, the man was looking right at him.

"No!" Dicky Parker said.

Clint hated back-shooters worse than anything in the world. The most horrible death that he could imagine for himself would be at the hands of a back-shooter, like the man who had killed his friend Wild Bill Hickok.

"Wait!" Dicky Parker cried, spreading his hands, the gun hanging limply from his fingers.

"I don't think so," Clint said, and put a bullet square in the center of Parker's forehead.

THIRTY-THREE

Clint holstered his gun and looked down at Andy Ludlum. The man was on his back, his hand behind him, pressed to his wound. There was no exit wound, so the bullet was still inside. He started to lean over Ludlum when a voice called out to him sharply.

"I wouldn't do that."

Clint stopped and looked at the man who had spoken. Apparently, he was also the man who had just saved his life by killing Dicky Parker's two partners.

"My friend needs a doctor."

"Well, then, he's just gonna have to have somebody else take him there."

"I don't understand."

"Sure you do. We're not finished here yet," the man said.

"Finished with what?"

"You and me."

"I don't understand," Clint said. "Didn't you just save my life?"

"That's right."

"Then why do you want to do this?"

"You deserve better than being shot in the back by a bunch of cowards. You deserve to be killed fair and square, by a man who's facing you."

"Like you?"

"That's right."

Clint studied the man. He appeared to be in his mid-twenties, and he was obviously very good with his gun. Clint had seen a lot of his type before, and had seen most of them buried.

"You don't want to do this, son."

"Why not?"

"Just walk out of here with my thanks and forget about this part. I will."

The man shook his head.

"I can't do that. I'm committed."

"What's your name?"

"Scott Bishop."

"Listen, Scott, a lot of men have tried this before, and I'm still here."

"Maybe it's time for you to be taken. Maybe the time is just right."

Clint smiled, an ironic, humorless smile.

"Believe me, son, I'd know if the time was right. I'd be the first one to know when I'm ripe for the taking, and this isn't the time."

Bishop licked his lips and moved his feet nervously, but he showed no signs of backing down.

"I'm sorry," he said, "I really am, but now that I started this I got to know how it comes out."

"Badly," Clint said, "Scott, take my word for it, it comes out badly."

"I've got to see for myself."

"You're too good with that gun for me to take a chance on anything but killing you, Scott. You understand that, don't you?"

"I understand."

"You're not leaving me any other choice."

"I don't mean to."

"Are you going to holster your gun?"

"That's the only way it'll be fair," Bishop said, and slid the weapon back into the holster.

The other two men in the room had ducked under tables when the initial shooting started, and the bartender had dropped down behind the bar. Now the three of them were sticking their heads out to see what was happening.

Andy Ludlum was lying on the floor. Initially he had felt pain, but now he just felt numb. He was looking up at Clint, but was unable to say anything. He knew he was just going to have to wait for the outcome.

He hoped he didn't die waiting.

Clint was hoping to give Bishop the time to back out, but with Ludlum bleeding all over the floor he couldn't afford to wait too long. If the younger man didn't make a move soon, he'd have to.

• • •

How did he get himself into this? Scott Bishop wondered. He could have just sat and watched Dicky Parker and his friends kill Clint Adams, and it would have all been over. Now he could feel the sweat rolling down to the small of his back, and there was a drop right on the end of his nose that was driving him crazy.

Abruptly he decided that when that drop of sweat fell, he'd draw his gun.

The droplet of sweat glistened in the light, wavered for a moment, and when additional moisture flowed into it and made it heavy enough, it fell to the floor.

It hadn't landed yet when the shot rang out.

THIRTY-FOUR

Sheriff Lou Baker was sitting at his desk when he heard all the shooting. His first instinct was to run out and see what was happening, but then he remembered what Peck had told him about staying out of the way. He sank back down in his chair and waited. He was surprised moments later when there was a single shot. After that it got quiet, and he finally decided it was time for him to put in an appearance and act like he was really a sheriff.

Clint wasted no time. He didn't even watch Scott Bishop fall. He holstered his gun and lifted Andy Ludlum up into his arms.

"Where's the nearest doctor?" he asked the bartender.

"Down the street."

"Where, man? Show me!"

The bartender hurried out from behind the bar and went out through the batwing doors. He led the way down the street to the left with Clint in hot pursuit and then stopped, pointing.

"This is it."

"Get the door!"

The man opened the door, and Clint carried Ludlum inside. A tall, gray-haired man with wire-rimmed spectacles looked up from his desk and, to his credit, wasted no time asking questions. He leapt up from his seat and opened a second door.

"Take him inside, quickly. Put him on the table."

Clint carried Ludlum into the second room and set him down on an examination table. The doctor hurried in behind him.

"Get out!" the doctor said, while washing his hands in a basin of water.

"But I can help—"

"From the looks of him, I'm not going to need any help. Get out."

It was true. Not only was Ludlum thin and frail looking, but at the moment he wasn't even conscious.

"You'll only be in my way."

"All right."

"You can wait outside," the doctor said, drying his hands on a towel, "or go and see the sheriff. He'll probably want to talk with you about this."

Clint snorted derisively.

"I see you've met the sheriff." The doctor tossed

his towel aside and said, "All right then, wait for me in my office."

"Thanks, Doc."

Clint took one last look at Ludlum, who was as pale as a ghost, and then went out into the office and closed the door behind him.

Out in the doctor's office he sat down and went over the incidents of the past ten minutes in his mind. Parker and his two friends had tried to back-shoot him. Both Ludlum and Scott Bishop had intervened—not that he needed the help. He thought he was quite capable of handling the three men. Ludlum, in his anxiety to help, had gotten in the way and gotten himself shot.

The other man, Scott Bishop, was a puzzle. Was he originally in on the back-shooting and changed his mind? Or was he just a bystander who didn't want to see Clint get shot? That couldn't be, though, because he obviously knew who Clint was when he helped him. He was, in fact, trying to save Clint for himself.

He wondered if Scott Bishop also worked for David Peck.

And what about Peck? Had he sent Parker and the other two after Clint, or was Parker acting on his own to gain revenge for what had happened in the street earlier? And if Peck sent them, what was the dinner invitation all about? Obviously, if he tried to have Clint killed, he would never expect Clint to show up for dinner.

Clint decided the best way to find out just what Peck's part in this was would be to appear at his

house for dinner and watch his face very carefully. He was sure that if the man thought he was
dead, he'd never be able to hide his surprise.

The first place Sheriff Baker went was the
saloon. When he got there, he spotted four men
on the floor, dead. He was not surprised to find
that none of them was Clint Adams. After all,
Adams was the Gunsmith.

"Where were you when we needed you?" the
bartender demanded.

Baker ignored the man. He walked over to the
fallen men and looked at each of them in turn.
He recognized all of them as men who worked for
David Peck.

There was a smear of blood on the floor in
front of the door, though, as if someone had fallen
there, wounded.

His next stop, then, would be the doctor's office.

THIRTY-FIVE

When the sheriff walked into the doctor's office, he saw Clint Adams standing there, apparently uninjured.

"You look disappointed," Clint said to the man. "Did you think I was dead? Or were you hoping?"

Baker frowned.

"I'm just trying to find out what happened," Baker said.

"If that was the case, I would have expected to see you at the saloon while the shooting was still going on."

Baker frowned.

"I came as soon as I heard."

"Then you must either be deaf or a deep sleeper," Clint said.

"I don't have to take that from you, Adams."

"Then leave."

"I got some questions to ask you."

"Don't ask me, ask Peck."

Baker frowned.

"Ask him what?"

"Ask him why three of his men tried to shoot me in the back."

"Three?"

Clint looked at Baker carefully.

"Unless that fourth dead man worked for him also? Oh, I see, they did all work for him."

"Well—"

"Then tell him this for me. Tell him the man named Bishop saved my life. He shot two of the three men who tried to back-shoot me. I killed Dicky Parker."

"And Bishop?"

"After the others were dead, he tried to kill me face-to-face. That didn't work either."

"And who's in here? Who else got hurt?"

"Andy Ludlum is inside."

"Who?"

"The man I came into your office with."

"Oh, the sodbuster."

"That sodbuster saved my life too and took a bullet while doing it. You give Peck a message for me, Sheriff. You tell him that if Andy Ludlum dies, and I find out that his men were working under his orders—no, wait, I got a better idea."

"What?"

"Peck invited me to have dinner with him tonight."

"He did?"

"That's right, and I'm going to accept. I'll give him the message myself."

"Mr. Peck invited you to dinner?"

"Yes."

"Why?"

"Because he thought I'd be dead."

"He invited you to dinner because he thought you'd be dead?" Baker was obviously confused.

"Don't try to figure it out, Baker. Just stay out of my way."

"Now look—"

"No, you look. If word gets to Peck that I'm alive before I get there, I'm going to come after you."

"Hey . . . I'm the law."

"I don't think much of you, Baker, not as a lawman, and sure as hell not as a man. I'll tell you one more time. You get in my way and I'll come for you."

Baker stared at Clint Adams, wishing he had the courage to stand up to the man—but he didn't. He probably wouldn't have even if Adams wasn't the Gunsmith, but he was, and that still scared Lou Baker.

The door to the doctor's examining room opened, and the doctor came out.

"Oh, Sheriff, I didn't know you were here."

"I—"

"The sheriff was just leaving, Doc."

"Is that a fact?"

The doctor looked at Baker, along with Clint Adams. The sheriff was not able to withstand the double stare. He turned and walked out without a word.

"Well," the doctor said, "you sure treated him the way he deserves to be treated."

"How's Andy doing, Doc?"

"Oh, he'll be all right. The bullet missed his kidney and anything else vital. I got it out. I'll wrap him up, but you should find him a place to stay in town for a few days. A ride back to his camp will start him bleeding again, and might kill him."

"I'll see to it, Doc."

"What happened anyway?"

"Oh, a few of David Peck's men tried to shoot me in the back. Ludlum got between me and the bullet he took."

"I see. He saved your life then?"

It wasn't exactly that way, but Clint decided against explaining it.

"Yeah, Doc, he saved my life."

"What does David Peck have against you?"

"I killed some of his men this morning when they raided Andy's camp. They killed a man, and I refused to stand by and watch them kill more."

"How many of them did you kill?"

"Four."

"And how many in the saloon?"

"Four more."

The doctor's eyebrows shot up. At that moment Clint saw something familiar in the doctor's face, but he couldn't quite place it.

"You're piling yourself up quite a body count. What's your name, anyway?"

"Clint Adams."

The doctor obviously recognized the name.

"I see."

"Maybe," Clint said, "and maybe you don't, but there's no point in me arguing about it now. None of the men in question gave me much of a choice. Can I go in and see Andy?"

"Sure."

"Thanks, Doc . . . Oh, what's your name?" Clint asked.

The doctor smiled and held out a clean hand. He'd obviously washed up again after treating Ludlum.

"Peck," the doctor said, "Doctor Leland Peck."

"Peck?" Clint asked, as if he hadn't heard correctly.

"That's right," the doctor said, "David Peck is my younger brother."

THIRTY-SIX

Before going in to see Andy Ludlum, Clint decided to talk with Leland Peck about his brother.

"There's not much I can tell you about David."

"But you're his brother."

"Yes, but I don't understand the man. He has this compulsion to . . . to own everything. I don't understand where it comes from."

"There are lots of men like that," Clint said, "but they don't break the law and kill people to accomplish their goals."

"I know."

"Do you talk to your brother?"

The man shook his head sadly.

"He wants nothing to do with me, except when he's ill," Peck said.

"And you go?"

"I must," the doctor said. "It's my oath, to care

for the sick no matter who they are."

"Doctor," Clint said, "through no fault of my own—I think—I'm at odds with your brother."

"I understand that fully," Dr. Peck said. "I think my brother may have found an enemy he can't bully."

"He found that in those people out at that camp," Clint said.

"Well, then, perhaps in you he has met his match," Peck said. "I must tell you something, however."

"What?"

"You may take offense."

"Don't worry about that, Doctor."

The doctor studied Clint for a moment before saying what he had to say.

"I do not approve of you any more than I do him. Therefore, I will not take sides in the dispute. It's between the two of you."

"I understand that, Doctor, and I don't have a problem with it. But there's something you should understand."

"Yes, I know," the doctor said, "you might have to kill him."

"I hope it doesn't come to that."

"I believe you, young man," Dr. Peck said. "I believe you. Now why don't you go in and see your friend?"

"I think I will, Doctor. Thank you."

Clint left the doctor sitting at his desk with his head bowed. Despite everything the man said, Clint believed he still loved his brother and was worried about him. He fervently hoped he would not have to kill David Peck.

He hoped he would not have to kill anyone else!

As he entered the room, Andy Ludlum turned his head to look at him. The man was deathly pale and could barely manage a weak smile.

"Guess I made it, huh?"

"I guess we both did," Clint said, "thanks to you. You pushed me out of the way and took a bullet that was meant for me."

Clint didn't add that the heroic gesture was unnecessary. It was made just the same and should be appreciated.

"I . . . I couldn't let them just shoot you in the back, Clint."

"I appreciate that, Andy."

"What happened to them?"

"They're dead."

Ludlum closed his eyes. For a moment Clint thought the man had fallen asleep, or passed out, but then the eyes opened.

"You killed them."

"I had no choice."

The man on the table nodded.

"I understand . . . it's just . . . so many people have died."

"You can stop it, Andy," Clint said. "You can keep anyone else from getting hurt."

"Me?" Ludlum asked, looking puzzled. "How can I do that?"

"Convince the others, convince Iris, that it's time to move on."

Ludlum closed his eyes again.

"I can't do that, Clint."

"Why not?"

"Iris won't listen."

"Then make her listen."

"How?"

"Don't ask her, Andy," Clint said, "tell her."

Ludlum managed another weak smile.

"Iris isn't someone you tell—"

"Andy, I think it's more a case of you not being the kind of person who can tell her what to do. You're going to have to change that. It's the only way to make her respect you, and then marry you. You do want to marry her, don't you?"

"Of course."

"Then you're going to have to make a decision, my friend. If you all stay here, Iris and Olivia could end up the next ones to die."

Ludlum's eyes stayed closed.

"Think about it for a while, Andy," Clint said. "I'm going to go and find a place to put you up, and then I'll come back for you."

Ludlum opened his eyes.

"We can't go back to camp?"

Clint moved closer and put his hand on Andy Ludlum's arm.

"The doctor says the trip would kill you, Andy. I'll have to find someplace for you and me to stay in town, probably the hotel."

Ludlum nodded.

"Will you send word to Iris and the others about what happened?" he asked.

"I will."

"Will you go yourself?"

"I can't," Clint said. "I've got a dinner appointment to keep."

"With Peck?"

"That's right."

"Won't he be . . . surprised when you . . . show up alive and well?"

Clint nodded and patted Ludlum's arm.

"That's what I'm counting on, Andy," he said, "that's what I'm counting on."

THIRTY-SEVEN

Out at David Peck's house, in his office, Peck was looking across his desk at Hank Dunn and Rick Shelton. Standing in a corner of the room was Jeff Duel.

"I need you men to do something now," Peck said to them.

"It'll cost more," Dunn said.

"I know."

"You'll pay?"

"Of course I'll pay," Peck said irritably.

"We need another man," Shelton said.

Peck looked at him and shook his head.

"There's no time. I need Clint Adams dead, and it has to be soon."

"The two of us are not a match for him," Dunn said.

"You admit that?" Peck asked.

"Of course," Dunn said. "We'd be fools not to. We saw what he did to Brooks and three of your men."

"Well, he may not even make it out of town," Peck said. "I have three men there who are going to try to take care of him."

"What do you need us for then?" Dunn asked.

"Insurance."

"What?"

"Just in case he does show up here, I need you and Shelton to make sure he never leaves."

Dunn and Shelton exchanged a glance.

"We need a third man," Dunn said.

"Oh for Chris—" Peck started, and then stopped. He gestured toward Duel with his right hand and said, "Duel will be your third man."

Dunn and Shelton looked at each other, and then looked at Duel.

"That okay with you?" Dunn asked.

"I get paid to do what Mr. Peck says."

"Can you handle a gun?" Shelton asked him.

"I can handle a gun fine."

Dunn and Shelton looked back at Peck.

"Does he get any of our money?"

"Duel works for me. I'll see to it that he gets paid properly. What do you say?"

The two men exchanged another glance, and Peck had the uncomfortable feeling that they were communicating with each other without saying a word.

"All right," Dunn said.

"We'll do it," Shelton said.

"Fine. Wait outside for Duel. I have to talk to

him. He will instruct you as to what is to be done."

"And when do we get paid?"

Peck didn't even know which man had asked the question. He took a brown envelope out of his top drawer and tossed it on the desk.

"There's half," Peck said. "You get the other half when Clint Adams is dead."

Dunn picked up the envelope, looked at the cash in it, then held it out so that Shelton could look inside.

"One other thing," Peck said.

"What's that?"

"That's a lot of money. If you decide it's enough and you take off with it, I'll have you hunted down and tortured, then killed." He said this in a very calm voice and regarded the men without expression. "Do we understand each other?"

"We understand," Dunn said.

"Wait outside then."

Dunn nodded, and he and Shelton left.

After the door closed behind the two men, Duel moved closer to the desk in response to his boss's crooking finger.

"I want Adams dead, Jeff."

"Yes, sir."

"If he makes it here, that is. Tell the cook to be ready for a guest."

"You'll feed him first?"

"I'll feed him and talk to him and maybe hire him. If he won't take money, you and those two idiots will have to take care of him."

"How?"

"I don't care how, just make sure it gets done."

"Yes, sir. And what about them, after it's done?"

"What about them? I'll pay them off, and they'll be on their way."

"Oh."

"Did you expect I'd want them killed? Good God, man, we can't kill everybody."

"Yes, sir."

"I'm not a bloodthirsty savage, I'm a business-man."

"Yes, sir."

"Now get them to stay out of sight. If Adams shows up, I don't want them to be seen."

"Yes, sir."

Duel left, and Peck sat back. He didn't get where he was by not having a contingency plan. If Adams got out of Lordsburgh alive, he'd show up here in response to the dinner engagement and he'd expect Peck to be shocked.

But it was the Gunsmith who was in for a shock.

THIRTY-EIGHT

Since Lordsburgh was not exactly a bustling center of commerce, Clint was able to secure two rooms at the hotel. He managed to half-carry, half-drag Andy Ludlum over to the hotel and put him to bed in one of the rooms. He also arranged for the doctor to stop in and see him the following day.

"Where will you be?" Dr. Peck asked.

"I'm going out to see your brother this evening," Clint said.

"That's kind of like bearding the lion in his den, don't you think?"

"Maybe," Clint said, "and maybe he doesn't expect me to show up."

"Knowing my brother," Peck said, "he'll have every contingency accounted for."

"I thought you didn't know him."

"I know him enough to tell you that he is rarely caught unawares. If you're going to his house, be very, very sure you keep your eyes open."

"Doc," Clint said, "keeping my eyes open is how I managed to live this long, but thanks for the advice."

"If you don't come back," Peck said, "I'll look after Ludlum for you."

"Thanks."

"Do you have someone to go out to the camp and tell them what happened?"

"No, not yet. Do you know someone?"

"I have a boy who does odd jobs for me. For two bits he'll ride out there and let them know."

"Good," Clint said, "here's the two bits. I appreciate your help."

"I just hope you won't be needing my medical help for yourself anytime soon."

"I hope not, Doc."

It occurred to Clint as he left the doctor's office that in hoping Clint wouldn't be needing his medical assistance he was somehow implying that he wouldn't be as upset if his brother, David, did.

Unless Clint was simply reading the inference wrong.

Before leaving town for Peck's house, Clint stopped by the sheriff's office. He found Baker sulking behind his desk.

"What do you want?" Baker asked. "Ain't you made a fool of me enough?"

"You make a fool of yourself, Baker, by living in Peck's pocket."

"Is that what you came here to tell me?"

"No," Clint said. "I came here to tell you that I'm going out to David Peck's house this evening. Andy Ludlum is over at the hotel, recovering from the bullet he took for me. If anything happens while I'm away—"

"You gonna blame me for that?" Baker asked incredulously.

"As little as it means to anyone, Baker, you are the law. If you haven't done anything at all since you put on that badge, you better see to it that nothing happens to that man while I'm gone."

"And if you don't come back?"

"If I don't come back, you can return to just being afraid of David Peck."

"It don't matter," Baker said. "One of you is as bad as the other."

"Just remember what I said."

"I'll remember," Baker said grudgingly.

His last stop before leaving was the hotel to see how Ludlum was and to tell him that he was on his way.

"I still think it's a mistake, Clint," Ludlum said. "Peck must've found out by now that you're still alive. He'll be waiting for you."

"Maybe," Clint said, "but that's a chance I'll have to take. If all goes well tonight, this whole matter might be settled, and I can be on my way."

"Is that what you want?" Ludlum asked. "Just to be on your way?"

"Well, unless you can give me another reason for staying."

"Oh yeah? Like what?"

"Like a wedding?"

Ludlum shook his head.

"I don't think Iris is gonna marry me ever, Clint. Not after I voted against her and came to town with you."

"Well, you never know, Andy," Clint said. "When she finds out that you risked your life to save mine, maybe she'll look at you differently."

"You really think so?"

"What you did took courage, my friend. If that doesn't impress her, nothing will."

"Did you send word?"

"The doctor is taking care of that for me," Clint said. "I wouldn't be surprised if she came to town when she heard."

"That would be something."

"With a little luck," Clint said, "I'll be seeing both of you later."

"Be careful, Clint," Ludlum said. "I know you're doing this for us. If you get yourself killed, I'm gonna hold it against you forever."

Clint smiled.

"I'll keep that in mind."

THIRTY-NINE

Iris McCain went over in her mind the argument she had had with Olivia earlier in the day. . . .

"I don't know how you can just stay here and wait," Olivia had said. "Aren't you worried about Andy, and about Clint?"

"Why should I be worried about Clint Adams?"

"You can't fool me, Momma," Olivia said. "You like Clint."

"That's nonsense."

"Maybe if you're not gonna marry Andy, you could marry Clint."

"That's more nonsense," Iris said. "I'm not marrying anyone."

"Why not, Momma?"

"Because I've yet to meet a man who could stand up to the memory of your father."

"Then maybe you should stop comparin' every

man to Poppa, Momma. After all, Poppa's gone
and you're still young. You need a man. Every
woman needs a man."

"I had a man," Iris said. "The Lord saw fit to
take him away from me. Besides, what do you
know about what a woman needs?"

"In case you haven't noticed, Momma, I'm a
woman too now."

"Then act like one and go do your chores."

"I think we should go to town and see if Andy
and Clint are all right."

"No," Iris said, "we'll stay right here. It was
their idea to go into town. They'll just have to
pay for their actions."

"Do you want them to pay with their lives?"

That stunned Iris. It wasn't a question she
expected from her daughter. In fact, she had
been uncomfortable with the entire conversation
which, she now thought, was probably why she
blew up.

"That's enough, Olivia!" she shouted. "Now go
and do your chores."

"Oh, Momma," Olivia shouted back, "when will
you stop treating me like a child!"

Olivia had run out of the house then, and now
Iris had no idea where she was. Yes, she did. One
of the horses was missing, which meant that she
had probably ridden into town. Andy wasn't here,
and there was no one else she felt comfortable
asking for help.

She stepped down from the porch of the house
and heaved a great sigh. There was nothing else

to do but go to town herself to find Olivia and bring her back.

Olivia thought she knew the way to town, but suddenly she felt as if she had gotten all turned around. Was she heading for town, or back to the camp? As if in answer to her question, a rider suddenly appeared in front of her. When he saw her, he reined his horse in. He was barely a year or two older than she was, and he was looking her up and down with obvious pleasure.

"Where are you comin' from?" she asked.

"From town, of course. I'm lookin' for a camp of sodbusters, supposed to be by the creek."

"I just came from there," she said. Knowing that the boy had come from town effectively told her where she was. "Keep riding that way and you'll come to it."

"Thanks. You headin' for town?"

"Yes, I am."

"Big doin's there."

"What kind of big doin's?"

"Shootin'," the boy said. "Some feller killed four men. Imagine that? Four men! Sure wish I coulda seen that in person."

"Why are you ridin' for the camp?"

"Got news to pass on from the doc. Feller from the camp got hisself shot."

"What? Who?"

"Don't rightly recollect his name," the boy said, frowning.

"Was it Andy? Andy Ludlum?"

"That's it! Andy Ludlum."

Her heart sank.

"Is he dead?"

"Don't think so. I was told he was shot, not that he was dead."

"And what about the man with him?"

"Feller what done the shootin'? He's fine, last I heard. Well, I got to be gettin' on. If'n you're still in town when I get back, maybe I can—"

Olivia didn't give him time to finish his question. She kicked her horse in the side and headed for town at a gallop.

"Durn women," the boy said, and urged his own horse on.

FORTY

Clint left Lordsburgh with Dr. Leland Peck's directions to David Peck's house.

"I've not been to my brother's house in a very long time," the doctor had said, "but I still know the way."

Clint was halfway to the house when he heard a rider coming from the opposite direction. From the house? Or just an innocent rider on his way to town?

As it turned out, it was neither.

It was Olivia McCain.

"What the hell are you doing out here?" he demanded when she reached him.

"I was worried," she said. "I had a fight with Momma, so I decided to come to town to see what was happening. I met a boy along the way who said Andy got shot. Is that true?"

"Yes, it's true."

"How bad?"

"He's not going to die, but he'll be laid up for a while."

"Where are you going now?"

"I'm going to see David Peck. It was his men who shot Andy."

"And you killed them?"

"Yes."

"But . . . you can't go to his house alone. He'll have you killed."

"I'll be fine, Olivia. Now you turn right around and go back to the camp, young lady."

"Don't you dare treat me like a child, Clint Adams!" she scolded him. "I get enough of that from my mother. I'm fifteen—almost sixteen—and I have a woman's wants and needs."

"Is that so?"

"Yes, it's so," she said. She gave him a cow-eyed look and asked, "Don't you think I'm pretty? You never answered that question the last time I asked you."

"I think you're very pretty, Livvy," he said honestly. "I think you're on your way to becoming a very beautiful woman."

"Well then?"

"Well . . . what?"

"Don't you want me?" she asked. "Don't you want to make love to me?"

"Olivia," Clint said, "this is neither the time nor the place to be asking that question."

"When will the right time be then?"

"When the right man comes along—"

"No, I mean when will you be able to answer it?"

Clint frowned. He didn't want to hurt the girl's feelings, but the only way he was going to get her to turn around was to tell her the truth.

"Olivia, you're much too young for me to think of you that way."

"But you think of my momma that way, don't you?"

"What?"

"You want to make love to her, but not to me, isn't that right?"

"Olivia, your mother and I have never—"

"Don't lie to me, Clint. I see the way she looks at you, and the way you look at her."

"Livvy, stop this nonsense. I think your mother's a fine woman, and even if I was interested in her she hates everything I stand for."

"No, she doesn't. She loves you."

"She doesn't."

"I love you."

"You don't know me well enough to love me."

"You just don't love me back," Olivia said bitterly. "Just say it."

Clint took a deep breath, then let it out slowly.

"Olivia," he said, "I don't love you."

She set her chin firmly and then said, "Fine, then I don't love you either, Clint Adams. I hate you! Go ahead and get yourself killed and see if I care."

"Olivia—"

She turned her horse and started back toward the camp, just as he'd wanted her to. He couldn't worry about the fact that her feelings were hurt now. He would deal with that later.

If there was a later.

He watched her until she was out of sight, then continued on to the Peck house.

Olivia rode her horse back about a hundred yards and then stopped. Clint Adams couldn't fool her. He loved her. He was trying to get her to go back so she wouldn't get hurt, but she had to help him. She couldn't let him go riding into David Peck's clutches alone. He was a brave and wonderful man, but alone he was going to get himself killed.

She knew a shortcut to the Peck house, and she would be there well before Clint. She'd show him, and everyone else, what a woman in love could do for her man.

FORTY-ONE

When Clint came within sight of David Peck's house, he was impressed despite himself. Peck had built the house within the bosom of the tall timber surrounding it. The trees seemed to reach almost to the clouds. The house itself had been constructed from that very same lumber, two stories high and probably large enough to house everyone back at the camp.

Clint rode up to the house and was met by a couple of men. They were dressed not like hard cases, but like lumbermen.

"Can we help you?" one of the men asked.

"I'm here to see Mr. Peck."

"Is he expecting you?"

"He is, for dinner."

The man turned to his colleague and said, "Go and check it out, Joe."

"Right."

"You don't mind waiting here, do you?" the first man asked.

"No, I don't mind," Clint said.

They waited in silence for several moments, and then the man asked, "What's your business with Mr. Peck?"

"That's just it," Clint said. "It's my business."

The man shrugged, taking no offense, and they waited in silence.

When told that there was a man to see him, Peck asked his man, Joe Doyle, "What's his name?"

"Didn't say, Boss."

"Did you ask him?"

"No."

"It's a wonder the trees you cut down for me aren't smarter than you," Peck grumbled.

He moved to the window, which was right behind his desk, and when he looked out, he saw Clint Adams sitting astride his horse.

"Well, I'll be damned," he said. "He made it."

"What, Boss?"

Peck hadn't been speaking to the man, but to himself, so he didn't bother repeating it.

"Let him come in, Joe, and then you and Ben get lost, do you hear?"

"Sure, Boss."

As the man went to let Clint Adams in, Peck looked out the window and surveyed the ground. Dunn, Shelton, and Duel were nowhere in sight, which was as it should be.

Clint Adams might walk into this house, Peck thought, but he'll never get more than three steps out of it alive.

Clint looked around carefully while he waited and then looked back down at the two men when the one named Joe returned.

"The boss says to let him in," Joe said, "and then we're supposed to get lost."

"Did he say why?"

"No," Joe said, "and I didn't ask, Ben. If the boss says get lost, I get lost."

"I wonder where Duel is," Ben said.

"Duel?" Clint asked.

"He's the foreman around here," Ben said.

"Can't find him?"

"He's usually around, but today we can't find him."

"Maybe," Clint suggested, "his boss has him doing something else today."

"Maybe," Ben said. "Well, I guess you can go on in, mister. Want us to put your horse in the barn?"

"No," Clint said, "I won't be here that long."

Ben frowned and said, "I thought you said you were invited for dinner."

"I eat fast."

FORTY-TWO

Clint rode Duke up to the house, dismounted, and approached the door. His plan to see the look on Peck's face when he arrived had failed. Now he could only hope that he could talk some sense into the man.

The door opened before he reached it, and David Peck stood in the doorway.

"I see you decided to take me up on my offer of dinner, Mr. Adams."

"Not dinner, Mr. Peck, but I did come for some conversation."

"As you wish," Peck said, backing away from the door. "Come in, please."

As Clint entered, he saw that the house was set up so that a person could see every room on the first floor from just inside the door. Off to the left was a dining area, straight ahead a parlor with a fireplace, and off to the right what appeared to be Peck's office or den. There was a window behind the desk in that room. No doubt Peck had taken a look at him from that window.

"I don't think we ought to play any games, Peck," Clint said.

Peck frowned and said, "I'm not used to being addressed in that manner, Adams."

"Get used to it," Clint said. "You've got four dead men in town, Peck. That matches your total from this morning."

Peck simply shook his head.

"I can always hire more men, Adams."

"Is it worth it? Just for a little piece of land?"

"I need that land, and I need that stream," Peck said. "Those people are in my way."

"Why not just ask them to move away from the stream, then?"

"Do you think they'd listen to reason after all that's happened? You know, I think I played this wrong from the beginning."

"How's that?"

"I didn't realize that trying to force them off would only make them stronger."

"They're good, God-fearing, hardworking people, Peck. They'd make you fine neighbors, if you'd only give them a chance."

"They have dead too, Adams," Peck said. "I think we both know where this is headed."

"What are you going to do, ride in and wipe them out? Women and children too?"

"They've had fair warning."

"I can't let you do that, Peck."

"I'm afraid you don't have much choice, Adams. You were foolish to ride in here."

"Why? Because of the men you have positioned outside? Three of them, I believe. One of them is probably your foreman, Duel."

Clint had a great feeling of satisfaction as Peck's face betrayed every ounce of his puzzlement.

"How'd you know Duel was out there?"

Clint didn't answer.

"You saw all three of them?"

"Yes."

"And you still rode in?"

"I was hoping I could talk some sense into you, Peck. Make you see that this could be settled without any more bloodshed."

"There's only one way this will be settled," Peck said. "First I get you out of the way, and then those people."

"How do you expect to get me out of the way?"

"The minute you walk out that door, you'll be dead."

Clint looked at the door, then at Peck.

"What if I don't walk out the door?"

"What?"

"What if I just kill you right here and now?"

Peck looked confused.

"They'd kill you as soon as you went outside."

"No they wouldn't, not without you alive to pay them. I don't know about your foreman, but I'm willing to bet those other two fellas are guns for hire. They won't pull the trigger if they're not getting paid, Peck."

David Peck hesitated, then said, "You wouldn't kill me. Not in cold blood."

"Why not?" Clint asked. "What harm could it do to my reputation?"

He could see from the look on Peck's face that the man was taking him seriously.

"Now wait . . . maybe we can deal, Adams. What do you want?"

"I want a signed document stating that you won't continue the dispute with those people over the land they're on."

"Do you think you can trust me to abide by it?"

"I'll take it to a federal court. They'll make you abide by it."

"You're a fool, Adams," Peck said, with some of his previous bravado. "Don't you think I can buy a federal judge as well as a small-town sheriff?"

"I don't know what to think, Peck," Clint said. "I guess we'll just have to find out. Now sit down and write."

FORTY-THREE

Clint followed David Peck to his desk. The man walked around it to get a piece of paper and a pen, but he paused to look out the window. What he saw apparently pleased him very much.

"Adams, would you come to the window, please?"

"What for?"

"Well, I don't exactly know how it happened, but I seem to have acquired some insurance."

"What are you talking about?"

Peck turned away from the window, and Clint could see him smiling.

"I'll step aside," the older man offered, and he did so with a little spring in his step.

Curiously, Clint walked to the window and looked out. What he saw was a man standing in plain sight holding a gun in one hand and Olivia

McCain's arm in the other.

"I now have that child's life to deal with," Peck said. "That does change things, you must admit."

"How do you figure that?"

"Well, it puts me in charge."

"Of what?"

Obviously Peck was annoyed with Clint's inability to gauge the situation properly.

"Of the entire situation, Adams. Come, come, don't be dense. My man Duel is out there with a gun to that lovely young girl's head. That changes things."

"Not a whole lot," Clint said. He turned away from the window to face Peck, who frowned.

"What do you mean?"

"You just told me your plan was to kill me, and then kill all of them, right? To get them out of your way?"

"So?"

"So she ends up dead one way or the other," Clint said. "What are you asking me to do, walk out there and get myself killed in exchange for her?"

"Make no mistake, Adams," Peck said. "If I tell Duel to kill her, he will."

"And then I'll kill you."

"But . . ."

"See? Nothing changes. You'll be dead, and your men won't get paid. Maybe your man Duel will be loyal, but I'll kill him right after I kill you. I'm in a position where I've got nothing to lose, Peck, and you put me there."

Peck clenched his fists and turned red.

"You bastard!"

"Just sit down and write what I told you to write. After that you'll tell your man to bring the girl in here."

"You're bluffing," Peck decided.

"Peck—"

"I won't do it," the man said stubbornly. "You won't stand by and watch that girl get her head blown off."

"Shit," Clint said.

Peck was right. No matter what the situation, he couldn't stand by while Duel shot Olivia, so he did the only thing he could think to do.

He turned to the window, drew, and fired right through the glass. Hopefully, the shattering glass would not interfere too much with the trajectory of the bullet. He couldn't break it first because that would alert Duel.

The bullet traveled true and struck Duel in the forehead. He dropped his gun and released Olivia's arm. Even Clint Adams was impressed.

"Run Olivia!" Clint shouted.

But she was frozen, in shock.

He turned in time to see Peck produce a gun from a cedar box on the desk that was probably supposed to hold cigars.

Clint pulled the trigger again and shot the man through the heart without regret.

Wasting no time, he turned, hopped over the bloody corpse, and ran for the door. As he raced outside, he saw two men approaching Olivia. When they saw him, they stopped and turned to face him.

"Your boss is dead," he told them. "There's nobody to pay you now. If you draw on me, you'll die for nothing."

The two men exchanged a glance, and then one of them said, "You killed our partner."

"I'm sorry about that," Clint said. "I don't know which one he was, but I'm sure I had no choice. I'd advise you and your friend to mount up and ride with whatever pay you already received. There's no more to be done here."

He watched them carefully, hoping that they'd take his word and leave. If they drew, he'd be forced to kill them. He'd already killed ten men, more than he could remember ever killing in a single day. He had no desire to make it an even dozen.

"Make a move, boys."

They exchanged another glance, then put their hands up, palms out, and began to back away. Eventually, they turned and walked toward the stable.

"Come here, honey," Clint said to Olivia.

She ran to him and buried her face in his chest.

"I'm sorry, I'm so sorry, I just wanted to help."

"You're a brave girl, Livvy," Clint said. "Your mother will be proud of you."

"She'll be mad."

"Maybe so, but proud too."

"And you?" She raised her tear-streaked face to look at him. "Are you proud of me?"

"I'm angry with you," he said, "but yeah, I'm proud of you too."

"And do you love me?"

He chucked her beneath the chin and said, "Don't push your luck. Come on, let's go and tell your mom and the others that they can live in peace."

FORTY-FOUR

Clint took Olivia back to the camp, where she rejoined her mother. The next morning they both went into town to see about caring for Andy Ludlum.

After the women had left Ludlum's room, Clint walked over and knocked on the door.

"So?" he said as he entered.

"So what?" Ludlum said, but the look on his face clearly stated that things had gone well.

"How did it go?"

"It went fine," Ludlum said. "You were right about Iris. She treated me different. I don't know— I guess with more respect."

"That's good, Andy, that's real good. I hope everything works out the way you want it to."

"What are you gonna do, Clint?"

"I'm going to head out tomorrow morning."

"What about today? What are you gonna do today?"

"Rest," Clint said, "just rest. My foot still hurts, so I'm going to keep my boots—my new boots—off for the whole day, then hit the trail tomorrow."

Andy Ludlum extended his hand, and Clint shook it.

"Thanks for your help."

"Don't mention it."

"You're not gonna get in trouble for killing Peck, are you?"

"No," Clint said. "Olivia backed up my story with the sheriff—not that I needed it. The sheriff's just as anxious for me to leave as I am to get going. And I think he's actually relieved Peck's dead."

Clint walked to the door and turned back to Ludlum.

"You're a lucky man, Andy. Two fine women waiting to take you home."

"Don't I know it."

When Clint left Ludlum's room and went back to his own, he was looking forward to a full day's rest. He was only there half an hour, though, when there was a knock on the door. When he opened it, he saw two women standing there, a full-bodied, dark-haired woman and a tall, slender redhead.

"Ladies," he said, "what can I do for you?"

"It's not what you can do for us," the redhead said.

"It's what we can do for you," the brunette said.

Before he could respond, they both put their hands against his chest and pushed him into the room. They pursued him, closed the door, and shoved him into a seated position on the bed.

"I'm Anita," the redhead said.

"And I am Isobel," the brunette said.

"Just watch, honey," Anita said.

He sat and watched as both women undressed. Isobel had lovely full and firm breasts with dark brown nipples. Her hips and buttocks were firm and smooth, and between her legs was a tangle of black hair.

Anita, on the other hand, was tall and supple, with small, high breasts that were as firm as peaches, a slender waist, and long, graceful legs.

"You next, honey," Anita said, and both women started to undress him.

"Hey, wait a minute," he said, batting away their hands. "What's going on?"

"We're here to see to it that you have a good time," Isobel said.

"But why? Look, if you gals are expecting me to pay you I should tell you that I never—"

"No pay," Isobel said.

"This one is free," Anita said.

"Why?"

"We owe it to you," Anita said.

"What for?"

"You killed David Peck, right?"

"That's right."

"Well, all he did was abuse us when we went to see him."

"None of us wanted to go back, but Madam Sande made us," Isobel said.

"Sometimes he beat us," Anita said. "We all hated him, and now he's dead. We won't have to go to him anymore."

"So we came to you to say thank you," Isobel said.

Anita put her hands on her hips and gazed down at Clint.

"Will you accept our offer of gratitude?"

He studied both naked women standing before him, his erection a painful thing inside his pants, and said, "How could I refuse?"

They climbed on the bed and undressed him eagerly. Clint had been in bed with two women before, but these women actually seemed to want him at the exact same time.

He found his mouth filled with Isobel's firmness while Anita's mouth roamed over him. As Clint pulled Isobel to him, sucking her nipples and sliding his hand between her legs, Anita's avid mouth found his rigid cock and took it inside.

As she sucked him and fondled his testicles, he thought briefly that this was exactly what he deserved.

Watch for

LETHAL LADIES

152nd novel in the exciting GUNSMITH series
from Jove

Coming in August!

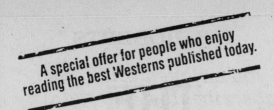

A special offer for people who enjoy reading the best Westerns published today.

WESTERNS!

NO OBLIGATION

Mail the coupon below

To start your subscription and receive 2 FREE WESTERNS, fill out the coupon below and mail it today. We'll send your first shipment which includes 2 FREE BOOKS as soon as we receive it.

Mail To: **True Value Home Subscription Services, Inc. P.O. Box 5235 120 Brighton Road, Clifton, New Jersey 07015-5235**

YES! I want to start reviewing the very best Westerns being published today. Send me my first shipment of 6 Westerns for me to preview FREE for 10 days. If I decide to keep them, I'll pay for just 4 of the books at the low subscriber price of $2.75 each; a total $11.00 (a $21.00 value). Then each month I'll receive the 6 newest and best Westerns to preview Free for 10 days. If I'm not satisfied I may return them within 10 days and owe nothing. Otherwise I'll be billed at the special low subscriber rate of $2.75 each; a total of $16.50 (at least a $21.00 value) and save $4.50 off the publishers price. There are never any shipping, handling or other hidden charges. I understand I am under no obligation to purchase any number of books and I can cancel my subscription at any time, no questions asked. In any case the 2 FREE books are mine to keep.

Name _____

Street Address _____ Apt. No. _____

City _____ State _____ Zip Code _____

Telephone _____

Signature _____
(if under 18 parent or guardian must sign)

Terms and prices subject to change. Orders subject
to acceptance by True Value Home Subscription
Services, Inc.

11049-X